RUTHLESS CROWN

Ruthless Royals Book One

AMANDA RICHARDSON

Ruthless Crown
Amanda Richardson
Published by Amanda Richardson
© Copyright 2021 Amanda Richardson
www.authoramandarichardson.com

Editing by Traci Finlay
Cover Design by Moonstruck Cover Design

This is a work of fiction. Names, characters, businesses, places, events and incidents are either the products of the author's imagination or used in a fictitious manner. Any resemblance to actual persons, living or dead, or actual events is purely coincidental.

All rights reserved. This book or any portion thereof may not be reproduced or used in any manner whatsoever without the express written permission of the author except for the use of brief quotations in a book review.

AUTHOR'S NOTE

Ruthless Crown is a high-school bully reverse harem romance. All characters are 18+. While it does not end with a true cliffhanger, there are unanswered questions still to be resolved in book two, which releases September 14, 2021.

Please note the trigger warnings in the blurb, which is located on the next page.

BLURB

Their names are whispers in the hallways.
Hunter, Ash, Ledger, and Samson.
The *Kings*.

Four of the most beautiful men I've ever seen, with cruel agendas and an even crueler reign over Ravenwood Academy.

Wreaking havoc in our small, New England town, no one asks questions.
For the most part, people ignore or avoid them.
After all, they're royalty here.

Because one of them—the cruelest one—is the headmaster's son.
And my new stepbrother.

They can try to torment me.
They can try to break me.

But they have no idea what I've endured.

They're used to getting whatever their ruthless, little hearts desire.
Maybe I should keep my mouth shut.
Maybe I should let them win.

But I'm not afraid of getting my hands dirty.
Lord knows I'm used to it by now.
My name is Briar Monroe, and these Kings are about to find out just how fucked up this Queen can be.

Ruthless Crown is full-length high-school bully reverse harem romance. It is book one of the Ruthless Royals duet, and while it doesn't end with a true cliffhanger, there are unanswered questions. Book two will be releasing in a month. It is advised to read them in order. *Please note Ruthless Crown contains explicit language, bullying, and flashbacks of abuse/trauma. It also features four hot AF guys who would do anything to protect their feisty Queen. The duet will have a HEA.

For all of the ladies who wished Buffy, Feyre, Peyton, Katniss, Aelin, Rachel, Bella, Rory and Sookie never had to choose...

1

BRIAR

"He must have a big ol' you know what," I mumble as the movers finish bringing our boxes inside the large estate. There seemed to be so many more boxes when we packed up our small two-bedroom condo, but here in the grand foyer, the actual number before us looks so pitiful. I swallow as I look around, putting on a brave face. As my therapist would tell me: *I can do hard things.* And moving across the country to a gigantic house I've never seen, complete with a new stepfather and stepbrother? Yeah. That's hard—though I'd never admit it out loud.

"What's that, hon?" my mom asks, a clipboard in her left hand. She's perfectly put together despite the hectic morning, her athleisure wear snug against her toned body, and her blonde hair pulled into a tight ponytail. One of the movers not-so-discretely checks her ass out as he moves a dolly back outside, and I roll my eyes. She had me at eighteen—the age I am right now, which is crazy to think about—so I'm used to people openly hitting on her and thinking we're sisters.

"Nothing," I answer, smirking as I run my finger along the dark wood of the staircase. The house—if you can even call the grand estate a mere *house*—is way nicer than I expected. *Go, Mom. Way to score that rich peen.* "Where's Andrew? I thought he'd be here to welcome us."

My mom shakes her head as she checks things off her to-do list. "Nope. He's in Saint Tropez until Sunday."

"How rude of him not to invite us," I joke, and she chuckles.

"It's for business, Briar. I wouldn't want to go anyway. I have so much to do around here." She looks around, and her eyes have that excited gleam she always gets when she has a new project in front of her. To me, this is a house—to her, this is her newest endeavor. By Thanksgiving, this house will be scrubbed from top to bottom, artwork hung, rugs placed down, candles set up on every surface imaginable…

"Mmm."

I look around. It seems pretty put together to me, but I know she intends to make it ours. Right now, anyone could live here, and the furniture and decorations are generic and dated. The foyer, which is where we're standing, opens up so that the formal living room is to our right, a formal dining room to our left, and straight ahead is the casual breakfast room, a library, an *informal* living room, an office, a kitchen, a wine cellar, and a conservatory that leads into the expansive garden out back, flanked by an Olympic-sized pool and tennis court.

And that's just this floor. Up the wide staircase by the

front door are *eleven* bedrooms. Downstairs, there's a large basement lounge area with a wet bar, a game room, a theater to watch television, another office, and an ensuite guest room, as if the eleven upstairs don't cut it. Who even needs that many bedrooms, anyway?

"Have you had a chance to look around?" Mom asks, pulling her credit card out of her wallet and handing it to one of the movers. They must be done. It didn't take as long as I thought, given the amount of time we spent packing up, but I guess any number of personal items in a place like this would feel meager.

"Briefly."

"Which room would you like? Andrew said to take any of them except the two at the end of the hallway."

I nod. "There are a few upstairs with a bathroom." Little does she know, I've already claimed the biggest room.

She mumbles something unintelligible. "Sure, hon. He made me promise to tell you that *mi casa es su casa*." She looks up from signing the receipt and gives me a soft smile. "He wants us to make ourselves at home, whatever that entails."

I put my hands in the pockets of my ripped, black jeans. "That won't be a problem," I quip, looking around. "The second bedroom is his son's?"

"Yes. But I get the feeling Hunter isn't here very often." She puts her card away and we both wave the movers off. Shutting the door, she turns to me and squeals. "Isn't this amazing?"

Amazing? Sure. My mom eloping with an older, rich guy? Great. After what happened, she deserves to be with someone stable. And being able to attend one of the most renowned private schools in Massachusetts because he's the headmaster is a convenient benefit. I think of what my life could be a year from now—living in Paris, attending university, eating croissants, outdoor cafés... *if* all goes according to plan, that is. I'm also glad to be as far away from California as possible. But I can't help the nagging, anxious feeling of being in a new place, when Marin City was the only town I've ever known.

"It's massive," I declare, looking around.

She walks over and puts an arm around my shoulders. Giving me a quick squeeze, she steps away and reaches down for a box. Relaxation is not in Mom's vocabulary. Doesn't matter that we've been driving for three days—now that we're here, there's work to be done. She's a bottomless pit of energy.

"Okay, time to unpack," she chirps, handing it to me. "Take this up to your room, please."

"Fine," I sigh, feigning annoyance.

I take the box from her and haul it up the sprawling staircase to the room I've already claimed as my own. It's the biggest one available, and it has its own bathroom, so those two things are a win-win for me. I push the door open and set it down. I have five boxes to my name, two of which are clothes. It felt really, really good to think about starting over here, so I didn't bring much.

I go downstairs and bring the other four boxes up, and I'm unpacked in a matter of thirty minutes. Mom promised a shopping trip soon, so aside from clothes, I have everything I need here. Photo albums, books, a blanket from my grandmother, a couple of sentimental knick-knacks, and then practical things like toiletries and accessories. I ignore the lump in my throat when I think of our condo, my friends, the fog of the bay area... it was my home for eighteen years. As I look around, I pull my arms around myself.

I guess this is my home now.

As I sit on the edge of the bed, I admire the shabby chic décor. There's a four-poster bed, chest of drawers, wardrobe, desk, and matching side tables. The window looks out onto the garden, and there's even a small balcony with a small table and two chairs. I envision sitting out there with some coffee, listening to music, reading, or just enjoying the changing seasons. I'm looking forward to experiencing a true fall, winter, and spring.

There's a knock at my door, and a second later, my mom walks in.

"Oh, this one's nice!" She walks over, sits on the edge of the bed, and puts an arm around my shoulders. "How are you doing, Briar?"

I let out a loud sigh. "Oh, you know." I nuzzle my head on her shoulder. "I think I'm fine."

She nods. "It's a fresh start. For both of us."

I close my eyes. "Thank god."

I love my mom, and she means well. We're super close, though I do often wonder if I was adopted. We're two entirely different people. Since she had me so young, and my father was never in the picture, we grew up together, in a way. Figured life out together. At thirty-six, she's still young and spry, and most of her friends are just now starting to have kids. She's the strongest person I know because of it, and still somehow manages to look like a model every freaking day. Blonde, athletic, a former cheerleader, she's perky and happy and is the first person to volunteer to help you out. It's no wonder she's a professional wedding planner.

I, on the other hand, have long, dark auburn hair, grey-blue eyes, and in the mornings before I've had my coffee, I resemble the girl from The Ring. I'm naturally pessimistic, sarcastic, and I've never done a sport in my life—I even failed out of physical education at my last school. I don't know my dad, but I assume I get all these lovely, cumbersome traits from him.

Despite our differences, I would be lost without my mom, and I know half the reason she moved us across the country right before my senior year was for my benefit. She saw me struggling with what happened, got me to see a wonderful psychologist, and when she met and married my new stepfather, the opportunity to move here presented itself. It seemed like a welcome change.

She stands. "I need to run a few errands, get the house in tip-top shape before Andrew returns on Sunday. Need anything while I'm out?"

"Maybe a cheeseburger?"

She snorts. "Two cheeseburgers it is." Bending down, she kisses me on the head. "Be good. Don't snoop around too much."

And then she's gone, leaving me to explore the house by myself.

2

BRIAR

While Mom is out, I do exactly what she asked me not to do, which is par for the course. Quietly stepping foot into the hallway, I explore the other rooms, most of which are just for guests. When I reach the last two rooms, I look around before opening the one I suspect is Hunter's room.

I've never met Hunter, nor do I even know what he looks like. When mom and Andrew eloped in Vegas after dating for six months, I wasn't surprised. I'd never seen her so giddy about a guy before, and it seemed he was smitten with her as well. Because of them being long distance, I'd only met Andrew a handful of times when he was visiting mom, and he'd mentioned Hunter in passing. I knew Hunter was my age, and that he was also a senior at Ravenwood Academy. But that was the extent of my knowledge.

We'd planned our inevitable move to Greythorn after they'd eloped, waiting until the end of summer to give her time to wrap up her existing wedding jobs in California. It made the most sense for us to move here since mom can plan weddings anywhere, and we were excited at the prospect of a fresh start. Andrew had offered to move him and Hunter to Marin City, but when we talked about it—and there were lots of discussions, because my mom wanted to be *sure* this was all okay with me—we'd both decided we'd needed a change of scenery.

I like Andrew. I don't know him very well since they've been long distance most of their relationship, but he's stable and boring, so that's good, I guess. Mom adores him for reasons I can't understand, but they seem like they're truly in love—*the real deal*—despite their fifteen-year age gap and glaring lifestyle differences.

Hunter's door creaks when I open it, and the bedroom inside surprises me. Black satin sheets, full bookcases made from black, ornate wood, a leather chair, a wooden desk, and a white shag rug on the floor. There isn't any art on the walls—just tons of small postcards pinned to the wall above his large bed. *Rio, Madrid, Copenhagen, Lima, Melbourne...*

I raise my eyebrows. I wasn't expecting a cool space like this, and I certainly wasn't expecting to like it as much as I do. I had no reason to dislike Hunter, but I couldn't help but form assumptions about him—like that he was a soulless, rich boy. I'd Googled Greythorn, MA, as well as Ravenwood Academy, so I had an inkling of the kinds of people who lived here. I'd already resigned myself to the fact that we'd have nothing in common. I mean, we obviously grew up *so* differently.

But... I would totally live in this room, and I'm officially intrigued.

I step into his bedroom and walk to the ensuite bathroom. Cologne and an electric toothbrush sit on the counter, and a luxurious black robe hangs over the towel rack haphazardly. I open the medicine cabinet, and several orange prescription bottles stare back at me. I pull one off the shelf and look at the label. *Lexapro.* Just as I'm about to check out the others, the front door slams from downstairs.

I rush out of Hunter's room and pretend like I'm just walking down the hallway casually. I cross my arms and glance downstairs from the railing, which overlooks the foyer perfectly. I'm just about to call out to my mom when four guys quickly jog back to the front door. They're all wearing black, hooded sweatshirts, and the one at the back has a bottle of alcohol in his arms. Though they seem distracted, I pull back a bit so that none of them see me. My pulse speeds up at the notion of being alone in an unfamiliar house with four strange men, and I wipe my clammy hands on my shirt.

"Let's get the fuck out of here," one of them says, his voice low. Another one laughs. Before I can digest their words, they're gone, and the sound of the door slamming again reverberates through me.

Maybe Hunter Ravenwood is *not* the unremarkable prep I thought he'd be as the headmaster's son.

I glance over to Andrew's room at the end of the hall. I walk over and quickly pop my head in, taking in the large master suite. My mom's boxes are sitting on the tufted bench at the end of the bed frame, and her suitcase is already half unpacked on the bed. When I walk into the bathroom, I see she's already placed her toothbrush next to Andrew's, and her favorite vase is on one of the shelves above the toilet. Smirking, I shake my head as I make my way back to my room.

I decide to go on a walk and stretch my legs after the long car ride, maybe check out the neighborhood... though something tells me it's just copies of this McMansion for miles on end. To say we're out of our element here is an understatement. I feel like I'm on a movie set. Everything is so clean, and the houses are all so stately. Even the cars are shiny and new. I didn't necessarily grow up poor—Mom's business brings in a decent amount of money—but Marin City is rustic, middle-class, and while it can be beautiful, it's also quite basic. I grab my Air Pods and phone, skipping down the stairs and grabbing one of the spare keys the housekeeper left for us. I lock the door behind me and head out, pulling up directions to the town center.

The sun is still high for being late afternoon, so I walk on the shady side of the street since my skin is vampire pale. I pass enormous houses with aging trees, and every few minutes, someone jogs by with a high-end stroller. At the end of the street, I follow the directions and turn right.

Of course, I researched our new hometown, so I know a little about Greythorn. It's a suburb of Boston so small that most people just pass through it on their way to nearby Salem. It sits between two large forests, so the town is surrounded by trees, making it feel way more nature-y than it is. It's also ripe with cemeteries and historic homes, which fascinates and intrigues me. Going from an overpopulated, California public school to a New England prep academy is going to be interesting. I know Mom is excited. She has high hopes for me since she never got to go to college, and she loves the idea of visiting me in Paris.

I round the corner and enter the main square, which has a large, tree-laden park in the heart of Greythorn with a thicket of trees in the middle. Shops and storefronts all face the park, and in the very center of it all is a large gazebo and lake. I walk along the perimeter, passing people out shopping and enjoying the weather before the darkness descends. There's a bite to the air now, and I suspect in an hour, it won't be warm anymore. I turn left and cross the main street, entering the expansive park. It's darker in here with the trees, and I hesitate at first. But then I remember Mom bragging about the practically non-existent crime rate in Greythorn, and I shake my head. I'm just being ridiculous...

I follow the dirt path deeper into the park, and even a few feet in, I can see the other side of town a couple thousand feet away. I'm safe here. But...

I look around, my spider-senses perking up. Someone laughs—a deep, cruel laugh.

I pull my Air Pods out and stop walking, listening. *I should be running.* I can't see anyone near me, but the eerie feeling of being closed in, being *watched,* makes me catch my breath. *I'm safe,* I tell myself. *I'm safe.* It's something Sonya, my therapist and I, have been working on.

Evaluate my surroundings. *A public park.*

Listen to my gut. *It's dark, but I'm okay.*

Apply common sense. *Just walk to the other side. Don't dawdle.*

I squint deeper into the thick forest surrounding me, and just as I'm about to continue walking ahead, a voice sends chills spider walking down my spine.

"Hey little lamb, come out and play."

The voice is male, reverberating through my core. I spin around, and my heart jumps out of my chest when I see four figures standing near the mausoleum in the middle of the park a couple hundred feet away. It's dark enough that I can't make out their faces—the sun behind them and the hoods shield that from me, and I clench my fists. Something tells me one of those figures is Hunter Ravenwood.

I ignore them and keep walking, my feet moving me quicker than before, and soon I'm on the other side. I look behind me, but no one is there, and I shake off the goosebumps at the sight of the four of them—lurking, watching me from the dark.

I finish my walk and get back to the McMansion just as my mom pulls into the driveway with cheeseburgers, fries, and shakes. I help her inside, chuckling as I spy decorative throw pillows and other miscellaneous items to make the home a bit more personalized. I'm sure Mom will bring it up to speed soon since the decor really could use a makeover.

We're both starving, having not eaten since we stopped for lunch earlier today, so we plop down on the nearest couch and devour our food. I manage to spill ketchup all over my grey sweatshirt, and I'm in the middle of dabbing it with a napkin when the front door opens across the foyer. I look up just as dark eyes find mine.

Hunter.

Some sort of quick recognition passes over his face. His eyes travel down my body briefly before he cocks his head, like an animal studying their prey. He's carrying the black sweatshirt from before, revealing a tight, white T-shirt that clings to his abdomen. He's tall and muscular in a subtle way—honed, but not outrageous. Dark, messy, wavy hair, and a face with a shadow of stubble and dimples. And his lips? They're full, tilted up on the sides, and cherry red.

I swallow. He doesn't break eye contact with me, smirking as he closes the door with one of his boots. The dimples in his cheeks are so much more pronounced when he smiles. He takes a few steps into the house, the muscles in his abdomen contracting with every step.

Lord. That is one fine specimen.

My mom jumps up and walks over to him. "Hunter! So good to see you." She gives him a quick hug.

"Hello, Aubrey," he says, his voice low and smooth. His eyes flick to mine over her shoulder, something akin to amusement flickering in his dark irises. "This must be your daughter." His words are dripping with something disingenuous, and my hackles rise instantly.

They pull apart, and my mom gestures to me. "Yes, this is Briar. Did your dad tell you that you'll both be seniors at Ravenwood Academy?"

His pupils darken as he watches me with cruel amusement, and I stop chewing. What the hell is his deal?

"Yes, he did." The tone of his voice is pompous, and his intonation is that of someone with a well-rounded education. *A rich boy.* How much does he know about *me*?

"Maybe you could show her around the school next week? Introduce her to your friends? Your dad says you're a straight-A student. Briar was in all AP classes back in California."

Please, Mom. Just stop talking.

"Is that so?" Hunter asks, smirking. "I'd be delighted to

show her around, give her a taste of true Ravenwood Academy spirit." I scowl at him as he moves to the stairs, but I don't answer. I won't give him the time of day. "Please, make yourselves at home." He turns to leave, winking at me before jogging up the stairs two at a time.

"Such a nice boy," my mom says as she sits back down, finishing her meal.

For some reason, I doubt that, because my gut is telling me otherwise.

3

BRIAR

I look up from my phone. *You've got to fucking be kidding me.* Sighing, I climb out of the Subaru and look up at the ivy-covered, brick edifice. Students in blue and green uniforms identical to mine file through the iron gate, clumped together in groups I can only assume are as ruthless as they were at my last high school. Luckily, I haven't seen Hunter since Thursday, when we moved in—apart from a very vivid sexual dream that left me all sorts of confused about my new stepbrother, but I digress.

I close my door and grab my backpack from the back seat, throwing it on as I lock my car with the fob. As I walk past luxury vehicles and fellow students with gold watches, designer bags, and diamonds, I keep my head up and eyes on the prize.

One year. I can handle this place for one year, and then I'm off to college. *Hopefully* in Paris.

I walk through the gate, ignoring the looks from other students, the curious gazes. My eyes take in the massive structure. This place is big enough to be a university. Four brick buildings surround the green quad, ancient maple trees scattered every few feet. My backpack thumps against my back as I walk to the administrative office. I glare at a group of girls as they snicker at me, but I hold my head high.

Picking up the requisite school laptop and a printed copy of my schedule, I head to the largest building—which I presume to be the library. I've never gone to a school that just gives its students computers, but then again, I've never gone to a school like Ravenwood Academy before. I have a few minutes to kill, and I might as well learn my schedule and see if I can orient myself.

I push the heavy, wooden doors open, and when they close behind me, I soak up the quiet and emptiness of the library. Inhaling contentedly, I stalk toward the back where several couches lie sprawling between two large bookcases. Just as I'm about to sit down, someone taps me on the shoulder. I twirl around.

"Hey, new human," a girl says, smiling up at me. She has short, black hair and golden skin. Like me, she's in uniform—white shirt, green plaid skirt, navy sweater with the white emblem on the top left collar. It's a crest with an 'R' in the middle, and wings on either side. According to Google, the symbol dates to Andrew's grandfather, who started Ravenwood Academy in the early 1900s.

I set my backpack on one of the couches. "Hi," I answer, somewhat surprised that she's being so friendly. "I'm Briar."

She shakes my hand. "Scarlett. And this is Jack." She

gestures to the guy behind her who is typing maniacally on his computer. "We're the nice ones," she whispers.

"How do you know I'm new?" I ask.

She laughs and points to my shirt. "Uniform rule number one: tuck in your shirt."

I set my computer down. "Shit," I chuckle, quickly tucking my shirt in. That explains the laughs. "My mom and I just moved here from California."

Her eyes flick up and down my body. "Okurr, I can sense that vibe now that you mention it."

Laughing, I shake my head. "I hope it's not that obvious."

She smirks. "No, it's not. Don't worry. You got that Cleopatra vibe going with your dark hair, but you also seem chill as fuck." Her eyes peruse my face once more. "They're going to eat you up," she mutters, looking me up and down. "I assume you're straight, which is too bad for me."

"Scar, are you seriously hitting on the newbie?" The guy behind Scarlett shuts his computer and stands. Walking over, he holds out a hand. He's tall and handsome, with red hair and thick, black glasses. "Hi, I'm Jack." He turns to Scarlett. "You're relentless."

I chuckle. "I'm Briar." As we shake hands, he wiggles his eyebrows. "She's not wrong. You come in here with your Xena the Warrior Princess vibes…" He eyes my combat boots. "Those are most definitely not adhering to the dress code, and I love you for it."

I look down. "What's wrong with the boots?"

"Oh, I'm sure you'll get reprimanded by Mr. Ravenwood. He's the headmaster."

I swallow. "I know who he is."

Before I can elaborate, Jack pulls out his phone. "Scar and I usually meet at the coffee shop in town on Tuesday mornings. You should join us tomorrow. Here, program your number."

I add myself as a contact and hand it back. "Mmm, coffee."

"Oh good, I've found another addict," he retorts, smiling. "This one's no fun."

"Hey," Scarlett whines, hitting his arm. "I like caffeine, too."

"Green tea doesn't count, sweetie," he jokes, shaking his head.

"Foul," I mutter, making a face, and Scarlett laughs, throwing her arms up. I point to my backpack. "I actually came in here to figure out where the hell I'm going for first period," I add.

"We'll show you," Scarlett offers, and I gratefully hand her my schedule.

"Ugh, history," she mutters, glancing at the sheet of paper.

"That's right by my first class. We can walk you over," Jack declares. Before I can thank him, he changes the subject. "So where in California did you come from?"

"Marin City." They both stare blankly at me. "It's the town on the other side of the Golden Gate Bridge, near San Francisco," I add, my words practiced.

They both *ahh* at my answer, and we continue chatting for a few minutes. Luckily, the reason for me being in Massachusetts doesn't come up during our conversation. I'm not sure how Andrew and Hunter are perceived here, and I want to get the lay of the land before I go telling people the headmaster is my new stepfather.

Just as I'm about to ask which classes they each have first, a loud bell sounds. I tug my backpack over one shoulder. They pull me along with them, through the door of the library and out into the quad.

"Just follow us," Jack offers.

"I'll give you a quick rundown," Scarlett starts as we make our way across the quad. "Don't make eye contact with anyone. Just focus on your own work." I swallow, but she continues. "Don't be intimidated. Most of them are just your typical rich kids, you know? Nothing special."

"Well, except..." Jack trails off. We enter the building to the right.

"Except who?"

They both halt in front of the first door.

"Okay, here's your classroom, bye!" Jack screeches, and then they're gone.

I sigh, looking into the large room where a few students are already seated.

Here goes nothing.

4

BRIAR

During my first class, I keep my wits about me, only looking up as the teacher goes through the slides. Lucky for me, being the first day of school, no one notices that I'm the new *new* girl. It's a big enough student population that I don't think any of them really pay much attention to me, anyway. There are a few snickers when I wander around the hallway trying to find my second class, but it doesn't bother me. It's going to take a lot more than that to break me. If the students here think I'm an easy kill, I prove them wrong with every glare I send back in their direction.

I didn't endure the worst nine months of my life for nothing—I was hardened now, safe from ridicule. These were kids, and I knew now that high school drama was nothing compared to the monstrous things adults were capable of.

Even though it's early September, the weather has turned cool, with mist and fog clinging to the brick buildings even though it's after ten in the morning. In a way, the fog is comforting, since my hometown is known for the beautiful fog. I stumble into one of the other buildings, tripping over the ledge of the door and catching myself before I fall face first onto the floor.

"Woah, there," Scarlett chirps, and I breathe a sigh of relief. She helps steady me. "Sorry, we tried texting you," she says quickly, and Jack comes up behind her. "We were going to show you to your second class."

"Thank you," I say, smiling as I pull my phone out of my backpack. "It's nice to know someone has my back. Literally."

"A lot of the kids here can be dicks. We're just trying to do our part," she replies.

Before I can respond, Jack grabs both of our hands. "Fuck. Here they come."

I look up, and it's as if the cluster of students normally crowding the halls has parted like the Red Sea. Four guys walk slowly down the hall, and everyone goes quiet.

Of fucking course Hunter is one of them.

"The Kings," Jack whispers into my ear.

I shift my weight to my other hip. "Kings?"

Scarlett sighs, whispering. "The Kings of Ravenwood. The headmaster's son and his three cronies." I glance over at the four guys. The hallway is silent now, and I have to try not to roll my eyes. "There are four names you need to remember: Hunter Ravenwood, Ash Greythorn, Ledger Huxley, and Samson Hall. The four Kings," she adds.

I chortle. "What's wrong with them?" I hitch my backpack and take a step to walk away.

"Everything," Jack whispers frantically.

I freeze. When I look around, everyone is looking down or away, averting their gaze like this is some animal kingdom bullshit.

I hold my place at the other end of the hallway, but Scarlett pulls me closer to her to make room for them to pass. The other students don't seem *scared*, per se—just aware of them. I study them, my eyes landing on Hunter first.

He's wearing the requisite uniform. Navy slacks, white collared shirt... except instead of a green blazer, he's wearing a fitted leather jacket with ribbed arms. It accentuates the muscles that somehow still poke through the thick material. His dark eyes find mine immediately, and something passes over his face—something dark and amused—as he, too, recognizes me.

I swallow and flit my eyes to the next guy. He's just as tall as Hunter, but leaner somehow, with short black hair and ice blue eyes. *Stunning yet cunning.* The uniform is perfectly fitted to his toned body, blazer and all. He's glaring at everyone he passes, throwing intimidating glances like he owns the place. A girl accidentally brushes against his arm, and he turns to face her while everyone quiets further, waiting for him to speak.

"Sorry," she squeaks out, backing up until she's against the metal lockers.

He just watches her and gives her a lecherous smile before slipping his tongue between his two fingers in a vulgar gesture.

Prick.

As they keep walking, I study the third guy. Long-ish blonde hair, edgier than the others, with tattoos peeking through the collar of his slightly unbuttoned shirt. He glares at everyone, an athletic jacket in his arms. As he walks, I see a flash of metal in his mouth. He's the only one not smiling and seems genuinely dissatisfied to be here. *Interesting.*

The fourth guy is different. Dark hair, fair skin, with glasses that perfectly frame his beautiful face. He doesn't seem as brutal as the others—like he's softer, somehow—or maybe it's because he's the only one not brooding. He's carrying a stack of books. When his eyes find mine, he stares at me for a beat and nudges the blonde guy. *Fuck.* They're both staring at me now, and Scarlett tugs me closer to her protectively—which causes my phone to clatter to the ground.

Before I have a chance to grab it and slide back into anonymity, Hunter squats down and hands it to me, the other three guys behind him. I take it from him, but I don't back up. They may have a bad rap, but I'm not afraid of them. The four of them falter slightly when they see me staring them down, and a few people whisper excitedly.

"Briar," he says, his voice like velvet.

"Hunter," I answer, tucking my phone in my backpack.

I'm just about to let him by when he takes a step forward, reaches out, and plucks a stray hair from my sweater—studying it for a moment before discarding it. Cocking his head, he doesn't move away—giving my body a slow sweep with his brown eyes. When they reach mine again, there's nothing nice in his expression. I swallow, and my heart races in my chest. He takes another intimidating step forward, and Jack gasps from behind me. I'm about to back up, but he grabs my shirt and tugs me impossibly close. Being this close to a guy, him *touching me* without my consent—

My head roars as I reach up and shove him backward. Just enough to show him that he can't touch me, can't *do* shit like that to me. He doesn't expect that because he stumbles backward ever so slightly. He narrows his eyes at the same time his lips quirk upwards, like this is a game.

"Don't touch me," I hiss.

He smiles and tilts his head, a piece of dark, curly hair falling in front of his face.

"What's wrong, *sister?*" The way he enunciates *sister*, the way it cuts through me like ice, *taunting* me... he's not going to make this easy, is he?

Scarlett audibly gasps. "Sister?!"

Rage fills me then, and I ignore the shocked squeaks from the other students. Heat flares across my skin, and my cheeks tingle.

"Screw you," I hiss, pushing past him. Scarlett and Jack follow me, and with flaming cheeks, I walk to my next class with them at my heels, ignoring the stares of every single student who witnessed our new sibling dynamic.

5

BRIAR

"I don't think anyone's ever talked to Hunter like that." Scarlett laughs as I link arms with her and Jack. We're back out in the quad. I'm thankful that they're in my second class with me, because right now I want to cry and punch something simultaneously. I'm going to need their support if these small interactions with my stepbrother continue to sucker-punch me. I ball my fists a couple of times to get the shaking to subside.

"Are we going to talk about how he called you his stepsister, or should we just ignore that fun tidbit of information?" She pauses and turns to face me with an expectant expression.

I sigh. "Fine. It's not gossip-worthy, though. My mom married Andrew Ravenwood." I pause and look at them, but they're waiting for me to continue. "It hasn't been so bad. Andrew is fine, and my mom adores him." I look back at the building we just exited. "I don't really know Hunter."

I think of his room—of the postcards, and the anxiety medication that made him seem like a real human for an hour—until he and his creepy ass friends catcalled me in the park. I don't know what I expected. Of course the headmaster's son is the leader, and of course he's kind of a bully. It's disappointing, but not surprising. He's a walking cliche.

Scarlett stares at me and twiddles her lips with her finger. "Rumor has it that Mr. Ravenwood threatened to kick Hunter out last year. But you didn't hear that from me."

I look between her and Jack. "So, he knows about Hunter and his..." I trail off. What, his *reign?* It sounds so silly.

Jack nods. "He's the eyes and ears of this school, Briar. Nothing happens without Andrew Ravenwood knowing. But technically, they never break the rules. They're just assholes."

"So, you *live* with Hunter?" Scarlett asks as we begin walking again, changing the subject.

"I guess so," I shrug. "He hasn't really been around much, though. He's out with his friends a lot."

"They go everywhere together," Jack whispers as we pass a group of students. "It's *kind of* weird. So that doesn't surprise me."

"I've known him his whole life," Scarlett adds. "He changed after his mom died."

I don't know much about Hunter's mother—just that she died a few years ago. I remember Mom vaguely mentioning at one point that while Andrew did well for himself, seeing as Ravenwood is a few generations old, his mother was the one who came from old money. Hence the McMansion.

"Well, considering I live with him, maybe he'll leave us alone now."

Scarlett's smile drops from her face. "There's no chance in hell, Briar. You awakened the beast. He's never going to leave you alone."

I swallow. "They don't scare me."

Scarlett throws Jack a look, but I ignore them.

As we walk through the door to one of the other buildings, a few people glance in my direction. I adjust my backpack as we reach our pre-calculus class. I find us three seats in the back, and the final bell rings, signaling the start of class. I prepare to endure the class in all its boring glory, sighing and attempting to forget my run in with the Kings.

An hour later, I'm still in the what-the-fuck-did-I-just-learn mindset as we walk out. They agree to show me to my locker, even though they're not really utilized now because of the laptops. Still, it'll be good to have a place to store things. On our way to the other building, Scarlett begins to talk to Jack about something animatedly, and I'm barely paying attention. I stop only when Jack and Scarlett stop walking.

"Shit," Jack whispers, glancing at the row of lockers in front of us. "We have company."

I look up and notice Hunter leaning against a locker, glaring at me. *How did he know I'd be here?*

Something fiery shoots through me at that gaze, and I notice Ash, Ledger, and Samson standing near the other wall of lockers.

"Let me guess," I murmur to Jack. "That's my locker?"

"I told you," Scarlett hisses. "They're not going to leave you alone."

I grind my teeth together and clench my fists. "This is ridiculous," I whisper. "I'm putting my foot down."

I stalk over to where Hunter is standing, arms crossed. "Excuse me," I order, not breaking eye contact. There's nothing kind in his expression, and his jaw ticks ever so slightly. A few people stop to watch us, their expressions stunned.

"You're excused," he muses, his face dripping with disdain.

My pulse speeds up, and anger flares through me. "This is my locker."

He tilts his head, and his eyes flash with amusement for a split second. "Yeah. I thought that was obvious."

Looking over his shoulder, I notice his friends watching me haughtily. *Okay, so they truly think of themselves as the rulers here, then? They sure have the arrogance to match it.*

"What do you want, Hunter?" I sigh, crossing my arms.

He chuckles, and the sound is both terrifying and thrilling. He reaches into his back pocket, pulling out a few folded pieces of paper. Handing them to me, he gives me a savage smile before I look down and take them. Willing my hands not to shake, I open the paper. My heart thumps against my ribs, and a flush works its way up my neck.

Snapping my eyes up to him, I pin him beneath an angry gaze. "You went through my diary?"

My diary—detailing the inappropriate dream I had about him the other night.

He crosses his arms and shrugs. "If you wanted me so badly, why didn't you just ask?"

Oh, the nerve...

"You wish," I growl, getting ready to turn and walk away.

Just as I move, he grabs the hand with the papers and tugs me into his hard body. Leaning down, his breath fans against my forehead.

"Tell me, just how wet did you get for me in that dream of yours?" To my horror, he raises his other hand, and a pink, lacy thong—*my* thong—dangles from his fingers.

My mouth goes dry, and my heart wallops against my chest as I close my eyes.

No. No, no, no.

Grabbing my underwear, I twist away from him and turn to walk away. Tears prick at my eyes, but I take a deep breath. I refuse to give them the satisfaction of knowing they got to me. Scarlett and Jack usher me out of the hallway, but before I get to the door, I feel a presence behind me.

"I told him not to do it."

I turn. One of the Kings—the one with the glasses—walks up to me. *Samson Hall.*

"He's lashing out. Give it a few days."

"You can tell him I won't tolerate this shit for a few more days."

"He won't listen."

I clench my teeth. "Why? Just leave me alone."

Samson laughs and shakes his head. "The more you resist, the more interesting you are to him, little lamb."

Hey little lamb, come out and play.

And then he turns around and walks back toward

where Hunter is still watching me, and the four of them head off in the other direction.

Was he talking about Hunter, or himself? I certainly don't trust any of them.

I glare in their direction, and Scarlett and Jack tug me toward the entrance of the hallway. I'm still fuming as I shove my underwear into my backpack. When I finally look at Scarlett and Jack, my pulse has slowed and I take a deep, calming breath.

"This is war," I declare, ignoring the look Jack and Scarlett share.

I have a really sickening feeling that this is going to be a long year.

※

Andrew Ravenwood calls me into his office during my next class, which happens to be my favorite subject—French. We're just going over the syllabus, detailing the class trip to Paris later this year, when I'm called into the headmaster's office. Scarlett and Jack aren't in this class with me since they're taking Mandarin, but I scoff at having to leave, nonetheless. I sulk the whole way to the main building.

I'd talked with Andrew last night briefly at dinner, and he was cordial, as he always is. I think he enjoys having my mom around, and he seemed excited at the prospect of doing family things together. I'd ignored the nervous pang when I'd realized he was referencing my darling, new stepbrother. I guess after three years of it just being him and Hunter, he was craving the true family dynamic again. I couldn't fault him for it.

I push the wooden door open, and he smiles as I walk in. Now that I've met Hunter, I can see where he gets his looks from. Andrew is older, obviously—over fifty, though I'm not sure of his exact age. He has dark, wavy hair like Hunter, but he keeps his trimmed short. It's flecked with silver, and his skin is a shade darker than Hunter's—tanned from his trip to St. Tropez last week. His eyes are green, and his smile is just like his sons.

"Briar, so good to see you." He's perched behind his large desk, and I nod at him.

"Hi, Mr. Ravenwood." *Mr. Ravenwood?* I've never called him that, but seeing him behind his desk, in a suit...

"Please, honey. You can call me Andrew. I heard there was an incident earlier today?"

Nothing happens without Andrew Ravenwood knowing.

I don't know what to say. For one, as much as I like him, I still don't completely trust men. After everything that happened, I just assume they have bad blood until they prove otherwise. Two, and maybe I'm just imagining it, but his voice almost sounds pitying. I assume he knows about what happened, and being a cognizant human, might realize my encounters with his son have been anything but pleasant. Still, I'm furious about what Hunter did. It was a violation of my privacy. So, I decide to go for the jugular.

"Yeah, there was. I think you might want to have a conversation with your son about going through my private diary." I stare at him, and he shifts uncomfortably in his seat.

"Right. My thoughts exactly. I will talk to Hunter tonight. We have a zero-tolerance policy when it comes to bullying here at Ravenwood, but besides that, he needs to learn to get along with you. You should feel safe in your own home."

I nod. "Thank you."

He leans back and watches me contemplatively. "Other than that, how is your first day going? Your mother and I were worried, after everything that happened…"

And there it is.

I sit up straighter and look at the clock behind him. *Tick, tick, tick.* "It's going well, thank you."

He waits for me to elaborate on that, but I don't. Like I said, I'm not sure I trust him yet.

After all, I trusted Cam, too.

"Good, good. I'm glad to hear it." He stands. "If you need anything—and I mean anything—let me know. We're all a family now, and I hope you know that you can talk to me."

Yeah—one big, happy family.

He gives me a genuine smile, and the ice inside of my heart melts just a tiny bit. I know he means well, and this is his way of connecting with me.

"Thanks, Andrew. I will."

I head back to French, attempting to fly under the radar until it's time to go home.

6

BRIAR

After my last class, I walk to my car with Scarlett and Jack, ignoring the four luxury vehicles parked up by the front gate. *Assholes.*

After the underwear incident, the energy at Ravenwood was different somehow—more frenetic. Like ravens waiting for the kill, the other students circled me, watching, and everyone we encountered whispered amongst themselves. I guess word had spread even though no one else could hear our conversation. They just knew shit went down. *Twice.* But I haven't encountered the Kings again, and by the time I unlock my car, I'm ready to go home, relax in front of the TV, and eat some chocolate. I quickly say goodbye to Scarlett and Jack, telling them I'll meet them for coffee tomorrow morning. It's nice to head home in the Subaru after what feels like an eternally long day, and I smile when I see Mom's car in the driveway.

"Hello!" I shout, waltzing through the door.

"Oh good, you're home," my mom yells back. "I'm in the kitchen." I walk to the back of the house, and my mom is sitting on the floor surrounded by plastic containers. "I'm trying—and failing—to bring a little organization to this household," she grumbles as she pours some rice into the container in her lap. "I'm pretty sure there were cans of soup that expired ten years ago in there," she mumbles, gesturing to the expansive pantry.

I laugh and sit down next to her, grabbing the pasta and beginning to organize it by type. I should've known she'd come in here and completely overhaul everything. While she gets her business up and running on this side of the country, I predict she'll be spending a lot of time bringing the house up to shape, too.

"You can definitely tell two men lived here by themselves for three years," she mutters, handing me the lentils next. I swallow at the thought of one of those men being Hunter. "How was your first day?"

I shrug. "You know. Same shit, different school."

She nods. "Yeah. Sounds about right." She turns to face me. "Did Hunter show you around?"

I stop what I'm doing and look down, wondering how to broach the subject. She obviously thinks Hunter walks on water and has no idea what kind of reputation he has. Sighing, I prepare myself to disappoint her about another man in her life, as if Cam weren't enough.

"Mom, how well do you know Hunter?"

She frowns. "Not well, I guess, but he's always been such a gentleman to me. Why?" I look away, and she nudges me. "Briar, what happened?"

I look down at my nails. "He's kind of a bully at school."

"Really? That's too bad. He's always so sweet to me," she laments, sighing. "Well, what do we always say?"

"It's always the nice ones," I answer, smiling.

That was our mantra this past year—the thing that justified Cam's behavior. The thing that brought us closer, like hey, *girl power* and all that bullshit. But it did help me open up to her, and as horrible as the situation was, it somehow brought us closer.

"I'll talk to Andrew about it later. Maybe he can talk to Hunter, really enforce some house rules about acceptable behavior outside of the house."

Pretty sure acceptable behavior was not *humiliating your new stepsister and asking how wet she got for you.*

I nod. "Andrew called me into his office to talk about it," I add, shrugging. "At least he's trying."

"Good. Do you want to talk about what happened?"

I shrug. "Hunter just needs to learn that I have boundaries."

Sonya would be so proud that I referenced boundaries.

"Okay. I'm always here if you want to talk."

I load the lentils into the container, closing the airtight top and handing it to her. "I know, mom. Good luck with this. I'm going to eat some candy and watch some TV."

"Okay, sweetie. I'll promise to talk to Hunter later."

I smile. "Thanks, Mom."

I grab a chocolate bar and my phone, heading up to my room to change out of the itchy uniform. Dropping the chocolate on my bed, I pull off my clothes, quickly walking into my bathroom to tie my long hair up. As I head back into my bedroom and reach down for the candy, it's gone.

"What the hell?" I ask, looking around. My skin begins to tingle with dread. Groaning, I pull on a pair of baggy sweatpants and an oversized T-shirt and stomp down the hall to Hunter's room. As I get closer, I notice music playing. I don't bother to knock—instead, I throw the door open and cross my arms.

Hunter, Ash, Ledger, and Samson are all here. Hunter is leaning back in a chair at his desk, his hair disheveled, his eyes on mine—smirking with delight. Ash is behind him, looking like an arrogant twat. Ledger is sitting on Hunter's bed with his phone, and Samson is reading a book on the floor.

"What the fuck," I declare, walking over to Hunter. He brings his hand up and pops a piece of chocolate into his mouth.

My chocolate.

"Sorry, did you want some of my chocolate?" he asks, his voice low.

I glare at him and contemplate swatting it out of his hand, but then think better of it. Why fuel the fire? I flip him off and glare at all of them before walking out. Just as I reach my room, there are footsteps behind me.

"Briar, wait," Samson begs, grabbing my arm and turning me to face him.

I pull out of his grasp. "What do you all want from me? Tease me at school, sure, but let me have some fucking peace at home," I begin, tears beginning to prick at the corners of my eyes.

I will not fucking cry in front of them.

I take a deep breath and stand up straighter.

"I just wanted to say, we're not bad people. Hunter's

just acting... ornery." His golden eyes watch me, and those dark lashes are captivating.

I cross my arms. "Why do you keep acting like his protector?"

Samson swallows, and I admire the way his throat moves. He's a beautiful asshole. *Why God, why?* In fact, they're all beautiful. It's just their souls that are rotting.

He doesn't answer me, so I continue. "I just want to graduate and move on with my life."

He steps closer, and I get a whiff of something minty. "Fight back," he murmurs, sending goosebumps down my arms and spine.

Without another word, he walks away, leaving me hot and conflicted.

7

HUNTER

Samson walks back into my room and closes the door. I glare up at him.

"Why bother?" I ask, my voice dripping with disdain.

Samson shrugs. "You're being kind of a dick."

Irritation rolls through me, and something else, too—some sort of possessiveness that I know is misplaced. Samson is the nicest one out of all of us.

Ledger laughs. "And that's surprising, why?"

I clench my jaw, but then Ash nudges my shoulder. "Come on. We all know I'm the real prick."

That causes me to smile just a tiny bit.

"Did you get the stuff?" Ash asks Ledger, who is still on his fucking phone.

Ledger nods. "It's in my car."

"Maybe we should stop messing with her," Samson suggests, shrugging, obviously still on the subject of my new stepsister. "Considering she lives here now and everything."

I look down and pick at a thread on my button-up. "But that would be so boring," I muse.

Something in my chest tightens at the thought of Briar and her mother being here. This is my house. Where my mother used to live. And they've just... taken it over.

Ledger laughs and shakes his head. "You're ruthless, dude."

I smirk. "You should know how much I like fucking with people."

There's a knock at my door, and then my dad walks in.

"Hunter? A moment, please." His face is serious and weary, and for a second, I feel bad for causing him to worry. He took my mom's death hard, and it was only after he met Aubrey that he started to feel like the father I had growing up. Still, if you'd asked me, meeting and marrying a woman he barely knew after only dating six months... I was skeptical. And bitter.

Ash, Ledger, and Samson are all quiet as I get up and walk out into the hallway with him. I cross my arms and lean against the wall, playing it cool.

"What's up?" I ask, playing dumb. It's not that we don't get along. If anything, he's a great dad. But he's strict, and I know I push his buttons often.

His jaw hardens as he loosens his tie. "I heard there was an incident with Briar at school today?"

I give him a dumbfounded look. "There was?"

He narrows his eyes. "Don't play dumb with me, Hunter. I know you're acting out because her mother and I..." He looks away. "I know you're acting out because of your mother, and the fact that Aubrey has taken her place."

I frown. "I was just teasing her."

"Reading her diary is more than teasing, son. It's unacceptable. She is your stepsister," he adds, his voice a little louder with frustration. He sighs and shakes his head. "No more hazing Briar. No more underwear," he commands, shaking his head. *How the hell did he know about that? Did Briar tell him?* "What were you thinking? I raised you better than that."

Yeah, until you forced me to cohabitate with the hot-as-sin stepsister.

Maybe if I taunt and intimidate her enough, she'll leave.

I don't say that, though.

Ignoring the pang of disappointment at the thought of her leaving, I swallow. It's been so much fun having someone to taunt, someone to take my frustration out on. I was so irritated at the thought of her and her mother moving in all summer, and then when I finally met her—when I saw her that day, out and about in Greythorn...

She wasn't what I was expecting.

Something inside of me twisted around that day.

Some deep, dark part of me was exposed.

"You may think that as my son, you get special privileges at school, but my threat still stands. We will re-evaluate your performance at the end of the semester, and if there's no improvement, I won't hesitate to send you to Jefferson," he adds, referencing the local public high school.

He'd given me an ultimatum last year. I was to do

better this year, be nicer, or he would uproot my life and send me to that shithole.

But then she showed up, and I felt... off kilter. I wasn't sure I could keep my promise to my dad before, but now I was more than skeptical with Briar around.

I look down at my shoes. "Fine, okay."

He jabs a finger into my chest. "She's your sister now, so start treating her like family."

I swallow, trying to dislodge the lump in my throat. The notion of Briar being my sister feels all sorts of wrong, but I suppose that's what we are now.

"I will try my best," I answer, giving him a winning smile.

"That's my boy." He pulls me in for a quick hug, kisses me on the forehead, and then walks off. "Oh, and you're grounded. I turned the Wi-Fi off for the night, so send the boys home."

I don't go back into my room just yet. Instead, I clench and unclench my fists, take a deep breath, and clear my throat before shaking the whole day off of my tense shoulders.

8

BRIAR

A couple of hours later, I head downstairs for dinner. I hadn't wanted to run into the guys again, so I'd stayed in my room and sulked, reading one of the books I had on my Kindle app. Crossing my arms, I walk into the casual dining area, and my stomach sinks when I see Hunter sitting there, chatting with Andrew and my mom. If they hadn't already seen me, I would've turned around and walked back to my room.

I'd rather starve than deal with Hunter again.

Glowering, I sit down next to my mom, helping myself to the chicken dish on the table. I ignore Hunter's gaze, though I can see him studying me from my peripheral. I begin to eat, and my mom clears her throat.

"I am very sorry for my actions today, Briar," Hunter grits out. "It was wrong of me, and I promise it won't happen again."

Anyone with ears can hear the sarcasm in his tone—the disingenuousness. He gives me a diabolical grin and tips his head in an apology.

I look over at my mom, and then Andrew, and they're both quiet and preening. It's obvious that Hunter got reprimanded and they ordered him to apologize, because when I look back at him, he looks like he's in pain.

"Okay," I retort, nearly rolling my eyes. Does he expect that a forced apology means I'll forgive him?

"How was the rest of your day, Briar?" Andrew asks, chewing his food. He's in jogging pants and a t-shirt—the neck damp with sweat. Does everyone in this household exercise regularly besides me?

I shrug, eating quickly so that I can leave to go somewhere else. *Anywhere else.* "Fine. I really like my French teacher," I offer, my cheeks heating. I don't like that Hunter is here—that he will know more than he needs to about me.

"That's wonderful!" my mom croons. "Briar wants to study in France next year," she adds, looking at Hunter.

His expression doesn't change—in fact, it doesn't seem like he heard her at all.

Or he doesn't care.

I take a couple more bites as my mom and Andrew discuss coming to visit me in Paris—anecdotes about turning it into a European honeymoon—when Hunter bolts upright, startling all of us.

"Goodnight, everyone."

He's gone before I can register his rudeness, and I swallow thickly before standing.

"I should go to bed, too."

"Night, hon," my mom chirps.

I wave before heading to the staircase, looking up toward my bedroom. I'm not tired—it's barely after seven. But hopefully Hunter is in his room for the night, so I can hang out in the basement until I get sleepy, which won't happen for several more hours.

Curse of the night owl.

The basement has been converted into a cozy, casual living room. It's unlike the rest of the palatial house, opting for comfort rather than style, with mismatched, oversized sofas, thick throw blankets, and the biggest TV I've ever seen.

I settle into the couch, practically melting into the soft, tufted fabric, when footsteps thud on the carpet. My skin erupts in goosebumps. I sit up straighter, and I don't look up as a figure in my peripheral watches me from the other side of the room.

I know it's Hunter without having to look. Only he can have such a melancholy presence.

I don't say anything. I just cross my arms and flick through the channel guide, trying to find something benign to watch. My whole body erupts in goosebumps as Hunter wanders over to where I'm sitting. Finally, I allow myself to look up at him. He's in grey sweatpants and a black T-shirt, and he looks angry that I'm here. My eyes rove down to his bare feet.

"Hello," I grumble, glaring at him. "Can I help you" I ask.

He laughs and rubs his lips with his thumb. "You're in my room." I open my mouth to protest, but he interrupts me. "I think we need to set some ground rules for the house, Briar." His voice is clipped, precise. Why does he sound so pompous all the time? "For example, this room.

It's mine, and you don't belong here," he says slowly. I *really* try to ignore the way the sweatpants hang on his hips, how if I look close enough, I can see just what my stepbrother is packing. My mouth goes dry as I shake my head. "You can arrange to have a tv sent up to your room."

I frown. "Oh, I can? How sweet. Thank you. I'll arrange to have the butler bring it up," I retort sarcastically. He's so accustomed to this life that he thinks he can just flick his wrist, and things will appear.

His jaw ticks, and he takes a step forward. Just as I'm about to ask him to leave again, he sits down on the ottoman opposite from me, leaning forward so that his knees just barely touch mine.

"This is not up for debate," he growls, scowling. "You're in my space." He's trying to intimidate me, but it's not working.

I frown. "I'll leave, but I'll be back tomorrow."

I begin to stand, but he reaches out and tugs my hands down so that I fall back into the couch. Leaning forward, he gives me a tight, cruel smile.

"Second, the next time you tattle, I promise it will be much more than your wet panties in my pocket," he says, his voice foreboding.

I glower at him. He's a rich, arrogant prick used to getting his way, apparently. But tonight, I'm too tired to duel. Standing abruptly, I kick the blanket off me and march to the door.

"I don't want to catch you down here again," he adds, and when I turn around, he's leaning forward and watching me with darkened eyes.

"You're an ass, do you know that?" I throw back,

narrowing my eyes. "You think I'll fold, surrender, give up —but it just shows that you don't know me at all."

He smiles then, and fury rolls through me. "I think I know you better than you think."

I clench my jaw and take a step toward him. "You know nothing about me," I hiss. "Or what I've been through."

My words cause his haughty expression to falter for a split second, catching him off guard. I wonder if he knows what happened to me.

I doubt it...

"Sweet dreams," he croons, winking.

He definitely doesn't know about Cam.

I twist around and stomp up the stairs before he can fire me up even more.

9

BRIAR

Scarlett, Jack, and I meet at Romancing the Bean just before eight, which gives us twenty minutes to socialize before we have to head to Ravenwood. The small cafe is idyllic, situated right on the outskirts of the park with outdoor seating and lots of plants. Scarlett's parents own it, and they're both behind the coffee machines when they introduce themselves. It's nice to meet them—to know that there's at least one other family in Greythorn who appears to be normal. Since it's cold out, we opt to sit inside, and I fill Scarlett and Jack in on my night with Hunter.

I swirl the liquid around and take a quick sip. "What exactly is their problem?" I ask. "The Kings?" Scarlett looks at Jack, and their smiles drop off their faces. "What?" I ask, frowning.

"You really want to know?" she asks. I nod, and she lets

out a resigned sigh. "There's a rumor that they were the reason someone killed themselves last year."

The words slam into me, and I think back to how they acted in school yesterday—like they were Gods who kept to themselves, who taunted anyone who dared enter or breach that fortress of power. Is it possible their behavior caused someone to end their life? Sure, they were mean—but were they capable of something that horrible?

"Who?" I whisper.

"Micah Smith. He was our friend," Scarlett starts slowly. "He was kind of like you—gave zero fucks, didn't care who knew it, and wasn't about the high-school drama and bullshit."

I let her words roll through me for a few seconds. "So, what happened?"

Jack shrugs, sipping his coffee. "No one knows for sure. But he started dating Samson Hall, and rumors starting swirling about a sex tape, and next thing we knew..." he trails off, looking morose.

Scarlett chews on a pastry as she chimes in. "Micah was already having a hard time in his personal life—his parents had just gotten divorced, and they lost a lot of their money..." She looks away, brushing a tear off her cheek. "He fucking hung himself, Briar."

"Were they ever found to be accountable?"

Jack bursts out laughing. "No, absolutely not. Micah's mental health history was a known fact, so blame could never be placed. But we know them—and we know what they're capable of. And the worst part is, they used it to their advantage." Jack looks at Scarlett. "They went from popular to royalty overnight. People bowed to them, scared of what they'd do if they retaliated or became their next source of entertainment. Over the course of a few days, people began to worship them—dressed like them, ran errands for them... We all knew the power they now held, and even worse, they knew it too."

"But they're just bullies," I grind out, fuming. "Nothing more."

Jack sighs. "You forget how impressionable we all can be. It's why we made it our mission to protect others. To take them under our wing and keep them safe. When you showed up—"

Scarlett nudges him.

I look between them. "When I showed up, what?"

"We knew you'd be bait, which is why we came on so strong."

I ignore the pang in my chest. "So, you faked being nice to me?"

"No, not at all!" Scarlett says, scooting closer. "But we knew if we didn't get to you first, that... Look, you're not the first new girl at Ravenwood, and you're certainly not the only one this year. But you're pretty, and interesting, and Hunter Ravenwood enjoys playing with pretty things." She looks at me with wide eyes. "I was just trying to protect you."

I look between them. "I appreciate you both looking out for me, but I promise, I'm okay. I've been through a hell of a lot worse, trust me."

They nod, and soon, we finish our coffees and head to Ravenwood. The rest of the day is surprisingly uneventful—and I only run into the Kings once, just before the second bell rings, so I'm gone before they can acknowledge my presence. Scarlett seems pleased that the bullying has stopped, at least for now, but I'm not convinced. The energy on campus still seems fraught with tension, still waiting for the ball to drop somehow.

It's the calm before the storm, and I'd be an idiot to believe they're going to leave me alone from now on.

I am sure the worst is yet to come, and I need to prepare for battle.

10

Briar

My mom is out when I get home, so I spend the afternoon in my room doing homework. We were given a reprieve yesterday, being the first day of school, but all my teachers had assignments for us today. Once I'm done, I take a quick shower before deciding what to make for dinner. I dry my hair quickly, pull on leggings and a sweatshirt, and grab my phone before exiting my bedroom. I'm about to pull the door closed when voices sound from downstairs.

Creeping to the railing, I peer down and see Hunter, Ash, Ledger, and Samson huddled near the front door, whispering animatedly. Narrowing my eyes, I try to decipher what they're saying, but it's futile. I creep down the stairs as silently as possible, and once I get to the landing, I peek around.

"...gasoline, it'll be too obvious." *Hunter*.

"No shit, Sherlock." *Ash*.

"What's wrong with a good old match or lighter?" Ledger drawls.

"We can't leave any evidence," Samson interjects, shaking his head.

They continue whispering, and I continue eavesdropping. *What are they up to?* Just as I'm about to make my presence known, they head out, slamming the door behind them.

I climb down the rest of the stairs and look at the front door. My eyes dart to my purse and shoes near the door, and for a second, I shake off the curious thoughts. Do I *really* want to see what the Kings get up to in their free time? And then...

What if I could gather evidence to take them down?

Maybe it's revenge for the journal, or maybe it's Scarlett's tear-stained face when she told me about Micah. If Hunter can't grant me privacy privileges, maybe he doesn't deserve those same privileges, either.

Either way, I feel compelled to see what they're up to.

If not for me, then for Micah.

I pull on my boots, grab my purse, and head out. Opening and closing the heavy door behind me, I slowly walk to the driveway just as Hunter's car drives away.

Not on my watch, assholes.

I start the Subaru and reverse out of the driveway as quickly as I can while still being subtle. I can see Hunter's black Range Rover at the end of the street, so I slow down until he turns. I need to put some distance between us, or he'll get suspicious. He drives out of town, toward the edge of the forest. I'm three cars behind him, and we weave down the single-lane road, through the thick trees of Greythorn.

Where the fuck are they going?

The car in front of me turns left, holding me up for a solid twenty seconds. I almost lose sight of Hunter's car, but then it turns right into one of the natural preserve areas. Slowing, I pass the entrance so I'm not *too* obvious. Hunter's car is in the parking lot, and all four doors open just as I pass.

Wonderful.

I make a U-turn up ahead and drive into the parking lot of the preserve, parking on the other side of the lot. The Kings are nowhere to be seen, but there's only one path into the preserve. It won't be hard to find them. As I exit the car, I grab my black windbreaker from the trunk. It's cold now, and the sky is light pink, nearly sunset. I shoot a quick text to my mom, sharing my location and telling her that I'm on a quick hike in the preserve. I put my phone on silent and tuck it into my pocket before starting the hike into the wooded, dusky preserve.

The air is cool and damp, moisture sticking to the ends of my hair. It's not raining, but the forest is dense, and the weather is humid enough that even in the cold, it feels misty. I slow my breathing and listen for them as my feet crunch on the dirt. I wish other people were around, but we seem to be the only ones.

My breathing turns ragged as the path starts to incline slightly. *Fuck this.* Why am I even following them? *Because maybe they're going to hurt someone or do something stupid.* I slow and look around. I contemplate going back home, snuggling up under my covers...

But then I remember Hunter's rules last night. How, even in my home, I am relegated to my room. How he thinks he can boss me around. How he *touches* me, despite me asking him to stop.

They deserve to go down.

And I need to be the one to do it.

I continue up the path a good fifteen minutes, breaking into a light sweat and removing my windbreaker. The thought of turning around is appealing, and I contemplate it again as I squint against the impending darkness.

Then, I hear a faraway male laugh.

The scent of burning wood wafts through the air, and I swallow, tiptoeing to the edge of the path. They're in the forest—talking, laughing, breaking bottles. I step into the woods, following the sounds and the smell of fire. Swallowing thickly, I pull my windbreaker back on, so I blend in better with the trees. A howling breeze has picked up, giving the forest an eerie, supernatural vibe.

After a minute or two into the woods, I see them. Four figures in black hooded sweatshirts... and the burning house behind them.

11

Ash

I grin as Ledger takes a step back, howling into the dark abyss of the forest like a feral wolf. When my eyes find Hunter's, they're alight with mischievous glee.

Good.

If anything deserves to burn in Greythorn—and I should know, being the mayor's son—it's this fucking house.

Burn it to the ground.

"I'm going to feel really guilty if the forest catches on fire," Samson muses, laughing. He takes a swig from a bottle of whiskey before handing it to me.

I sip the fiery liquid, trying to pace myself. There will be repercussions if I come home drunk again.

"The forest won't catch on fire," Hunter muses. "We took precautions."

It's true. As much as we wanted to do this, we were

also careful about it. We may be dicks, but at least we were safe. We waited for a cooler day, we waited for evening, low wind, and lots of moisture. I yelp and throw the nearly empty bottle into the fire, and it causes a small uproar of flames.

"Fuck this house." I dig in my pocket for a cigarette. I don't smoke that often anymore, but tonight feels like the perfect occasion. Samson walks over and lights it for me, his eyes on mine for a second too long as I inhale the heady smoke. "Let's fuck this shit up."

"Fuck this house," Samson echoes.

"Fuck this fucking house," Ledger chimes in, taking an empty beer bottle and throwing it into the flames.

We turn to Hunter, who walks up to the billowing smoke, the flames nearly licking the skin of his arms. For a second, we remember—the body, haphazardly dumped here, the way the town grieved, the way people expected Hunter, then a gangly fifteen-year-old, to cope with the gruesome death of his mother. His best friend.

He was never the same.

Taking something metal from his pocket, he kisses it before throwing it into the fire, and I realize it's his mother's locket.

We may think we're up here drinking, having a good time, but for him?

This is a goddamned funeral.

12

BRIAR

My pulse quickens as I walk up to the clearing, the scene coming into view before me. Drinking, lighting shit on fire, throwing glass into the flames. I don't understand the reason, but then again, I don't pretend to know what they're thinking or why they act like pricks most of the time. The four *Kings*, once again pretending that the rules don't apply to them. Committing *arson*. Acting like fools. I grimace as a cloud of smoke smothers me, engulfing my throat with ashy dust. Before I can stop myself, I cough.

Ash spies me first, his head snapping toward me. My stomach clenches when his smile spreads, an evil grin on his beautiful face.

"Well, well, well," he sneers, turning and walking toward me. "Looks like the little lamb wants to come and play, after all."

The other three follow his gaze and their eyes land on

me. I stand up straighter, balling my fists as I take a step forward.

"You're all idiots," I yell, looking at Ash specifically. "You guys could burn this whole forest down."

"So?" Ledger asks, taking a threatening step forward. He looks at the other guys with a wolfish grin, and they all nod. "What are you going to do about it?"

"Tell someone," I declare, crossing my arms. The crinkling of the windbreaker is drowned out by the roaring of flames. *Jesus, I hope they can put it out safely.*

"Are you sure you want to find out what would happen if you tattled?" Ash leers, baring his teeth as he saunters up to me. "Again?" He reaches out and plays with my zipper.

I jump back. "Don't touch me," I growl.

"Leave her alone," Hunter says from behind them all. His voice is calm, eerie—*practiced*. While the other guys are immature and callous, Hunter is smooth-talking, and his heart as dark as they come.

Like a psychopath.

Ash takes a few steps back as Hunter comes into view. My god—even as criminals, even as the assholes that they are, they're gorgeous. Hunter with his dark, mysterious swagger. Ash with his confident arrogance. Ledger with his brooding, bad boy vibes. And Samson—the quiet, hot nerd. Apart, they'd stand out in a crowd. But together? They're a force to be reckoned with, and for a second, my confidence wavers. The *Kings* of Ravenwood Academy. Royal, feared, powerful. I can feel it rolling off them, too. The internal light within them, the way they *know* they can get away with anything, *do* anything.

Gods. They're gods in human bodies. Omnipotent. Invincible.

To think I could take them down alone...

"You won't tattle, little lamb," Hunter muses, rolling his tongue along the inside of his cheek. "You forget that I know where you sleep. The things I could do would rival your worst nightmares."

The words cause my legs to wobble a bit, my core to clench. I glare at him, tamping down the small inkling of fear spider-walking up my spine. I want to say he could never do the monstrous things I'd experienced before, but as I look at them all, their eyes gleaming... I wouldn't put it past them. Men are men, and except for a few of them, they're all the same.

"Why the fuck do you all keep calling me a little lamb?" I ask, zipping my jacket up again as a cool breeze blows the smoke away.

"St. Augustine's sermon," he answers. "I knew public schools in California were abysmal, but I had no idea they didn't teach you basic history," he mocks, and the other guys laugh.

My cheeks flame. "I know who St. Augustine is, you idiot," I retort.

Hunter takes another couple of steps forward until he's standing right in front of me. "The lion is Christ resurrected, and the lamb is his sacrifice." He brushes a stray hair out of my face, his fingers grazing my jawline. Instead of immediately slapping his hand away, I stare up into his dark, soulful eyes. The flames dance in his dark irises, and I'm mesmerized. "*He endured death as a lamb; he devoured it as a lion.*"

I close my eyes for a second—just a mere second—and I hate myself for faltering. Hunter notices, chuckling. I take a step back.

"Talk to me like a normal person, not like the rich snob that you are. Explain why I'm the lamb."

"Don't you get it?" he murmurs, backing me up against a tree. His hard body presses into mine, and I inhale the scent of vetiver—from the fancy cologne he wears.

Run. I should run. Nothing good can come from taunting them like this.

"Get what?" I ask, my voice harsh and impatient.

"You're all talk, Briar. We are the lions, and you are the lamb. And we're going to tear you apart, piece by piece. People want to believe the lion will lie with the lamb, but that's not realistic," he murmurs, his face inches from mine. I want to push him away, hit him, put him in his place—but I'm frozen. "We are not of the same breed," he adds, and then his nose grazes mine. My eyes flutter closed. "And we never will be."

Before I even open my eyes, he's gone.

I blink a few times and look around, and Hunter is walking backward, an irritated expression on his face.

"Go home, Briar. And don't even think of telling anyone what you saw tonight."

This time, I don't protest.

I make it home just before Mom, but since I still feel rattled, confused, conflicted... I head straight to my room. Around midnight, the front door slams, and I hold my breath as Hunter's heavy footsteps walk down the hallway. I wait to see if they pause at my door, but they don't falter in their cadence. His door closes and I exhale, relief rolling through my body.

13

BRIAR

By the time I park at Ravenwood Academy the next morning, my mind is fuzzy with exhaustion. I slept like shit last night, tossing and turning, eventually dreaming about how Hunter's body collided with mine. I woke up frenzied and irritable, and the double shot latte my mom made me with Andrew's fancy espresso machine did nothing to cure my bad mood. I saunter up to Scarlett, and she can immediately tell that something's wrong.

"Spill," Scarlett demands as we sit at one of the tables in the quad. It's surprisingly warm today, and the sun is already out. She hands me a croissant, and I swear, if pastries could turn moods around, this would do the trick.

"You are a goddess," I croon, squeezing her hand. "Thank you."

"You're welcome," she smiles, chewing on her own croissant.

I lean back and let the rare warmth shine down on my face and neck. "I would love to open up my own café one day. In Paris. Maybe sell macarons and croissants like this, make fancy coffee... I'm applying to the Sorbonne in Paris for college," I admit.

She punches my shoulder gently. "Shut. Up!"

I nod and giggle. "Yeah. Who knows if I'll get in? I speak French conversationally, but being fluent enough to take classes in French..." I look down. "And then being able to afford it..."

She groans. "I feel you on that. I think we may be the only ones here *not* getting a full ride to college on Mommy and Daddy's dime."

I crumple the pastry paper and shrug. "Yeah, but that means we will actually enjoy college. Because we'll have earned it. Where do you want to go?"

She shrugs. "Boston University is the only way I can save money by living at home," she says glumly. "I'd love to go to Paris, though. Or New York. Or London..."

"That would be incredible."

We're both quiet as we watch the other students stand around, clutching their Louis Vuitton's and showing off their Rolexes. Scarlett and I seem to be on the same wavelength, because she laughs.

"Jack is filthy rich," she adds, nudging my shoulder as he approaches. "But he doesn't like to talk about it. He says he'd rather pretend to be poor."

We dissolve into a fit of laughter as he sits across from us, and we chat for a few minutes before the bell rings.

I manage to circumvent Hunter and the gang for most of the morning. I change for gym and walk out of the locker room, dreading the fact that I must attempt athleticism. We're outside in the state-of-the-art track that looks nicer than most professional football fields you see on television. The other girls look cute and stylish in their gym shorts. I just look like a bridge troll. Rolling my eyes, I walk over to where the coach is beginning to instruct us on how to run a mile.

Sure. Let me just casually run *a freaking MILE.*

I grimace as he blows the whistle, wishing more than anything that I had Jack or Scarlett here to help me through this. I can't afford to fail out of gym—which I almost did in California. I need straight As for the Sorbonne. Sucking it up, I start slowly, building my pace bit by bit, my feet pounding on the firm ground of the track. A couple of seconds later, Ledger wanders up to me, looking like a dark, tortured god with tan, well-muscled legs.

"Didn't realize you were in this class," I say glumly, and even barking out that sentence is an effort. I begin to breathe heavier, and I'm barely one-hundred meters into the run.

"It's your lucky day," he says, keeping his pace with mine. His tongue ring slides around inside his mouth, glinting in the sunlight.

I ignore him and try to focus on *not dying*. We jog side by side the entirety of a lap, and I try not to let him see just how out of breath I am.

Is it possible to die of a heart attack if you run too hard? Because that's where I'm at.

"You know, some people just aren't built for running," he muses as we pass the marker.

I stop and glare at him, my chest rising and falling quickly. "Screw you, Ledger." Sweat is dripping down the back of my neck. God, how can anyone possibly enjoy this?

"Just a word of advice... you're running with your toes up," he says, pausing next to me and pulling his shirt off. *Holy mother of...*

I look up at his face, trying not to stare at his sculpted-like-a-statue abdomen with dark whirls of ink that creep up to his chest and neck.

I'm practically wheezing as I respond. "What?"

He walks up to me, his lopsided smile taking me by surprise. "You're running with your toes up when you should be running on the middle of your foot." He bends down and takes my sneaker, tapping the middle of my arch. "You're going to injure yourself if you keep landing on your heel. Mid-foot will absorb most of the shock." He sets my foot down and stands. "You want to land completely flat."

I wipe the sweat from my brow. I don't know why he's being nice to me. "Thanks."

He winks. "And maybe consider swimming or something instead."

Ah, there it is.

My cheeks flame as he jogs off effortlessly.

I get back to the locker room and grab a towel, taking my clothes off and *still* trying to catch my breath. Of course coach was timing us, and *of course* I was last, but at least I finished. Fifteen minutes and twelve seconds. I walk over to the showers, washing my hair and body quickly before heading to the area with blow dryers. At my last school, we had sturdy wooden benches to get ready. Ravenwood Academy has a state-of-the-art gym—with a sauna, steam room, and a locker room equipped with blow dryers, deodorant, dry shampoo, straighteners, curling irons, and face wipes... you name it. I sit down and dry my hair, running a straightener through it.

I feel great—maybe running *does* have its perks. The exhaustion from earlier is gone, replaced by some sort of euphoria I can only assume are the endorphins everyone talks about.

My mom—Athletic Barbie herself—is going to be so proud.

When I get back to my locker, I pull my clothes on, searching for my sweater and my blouse. I pause. Checking that I have the right aisle, I look again, my heart beating faster as I realize my tops are gone. My heart thumps in my throat, and I look around to see if there's an easy explanation, but I already know who did it. There are a few other girls hanging around, getting ready in front of the mirrors, but it wasn't them.

Shaking my head slowly, I walk through the locker room in my skirt and my bra, holding my head up high, nonplussed. Seems as though Ledger's friendliness on the track today was fueled by an ulterior motive, or perhaps a distraction. I let my guard down just a tiny bit—assuming the *women's* locker room would be safe.

But I forgot who they are.

What they are.

I grind my teeth as I walk toward campus, hoping I can find Scarlett and Jack easily. I know once I find them, I'll be fine, and Scarlett will get me sorted. I can't afford to miss my next class and get a truancy.

I don't have time for this bullshit.

The eyes of the other students are on me. People stare at me with mouths agape, eyebrows raised, and a few of them even laugh out loud. My cheeks are burning, and for a second I want to run and hide and never come back.

But if I did that, they would win.

They don't deserve to see me rattled, and they don't deserve my compliance and my silence.

They can try to break me.

They can keep tormenting me.

I know this certainly won't be the last time.

But as I walk through the halls in just my bra, I vow to never give them the satisfaction of feeling like they won.

I've been through too much, endured enough bullshit. It's quite comical how much effort they're going through just to get me to bend to their will.

It's never going to happen.

My bare feet slap against the linoleum, and I stare at anyone who dares to snicker or giggle at my expense. I push the door open to the quad, and within seconds, I spy the Kings walking in my direction. Hunter stops and stares at me, his eyes roving over the bare skin of my stomach and chest like a predator assessing its bait. Ash whistles through his fingers and unabashedly checks me out. Ledger gives me a small smile and winks, and then he holds his other hand out with my shirt and sweater in his hand. *Fucking bastard.* Samson is the only one who seems a little concerned.

I am out of fucks to give.

Hunter chuckles. "Did you lose your shirt, sister?"

My throat constricts. Ash and Ledger are smirking at

me. Samson's expression is unreadable, but he doesn't look happy to see me without a shirt.

Ledger walks up to me and discards my shirt and sweater onto the concrete. It lays in a heap on the ground, and I clench my fists as fiery rage burns through me. A group of people begin circling us, watching, and I snap.

I take a step forward and shove Hunter backward as hard as I can. "You think you can break me?" I taunt, baring my teeth. "That forcing me to walk out of the locker room in my bra will cause me to bend to your will and submit?"

"Briar," Samson warns.

I turn to face him. "Stop acting like the nice one, Samson. You're just as bad as them. Maybe even worse, because people want to let their guard down around you."

He goes quiet, looking down at the ground, his jaw ticking.

"Is that all you've got?" Hunter muses, his arms crossed. His lips quirk to one side and he raises his eyebrows, an amused expression on his face.

I hate them.

I reach down and grab my shirt, pulling it on and buttoning it quickly. When I'm done, I look up at Hunter.

"Keep pushing me, I dare you."

"Yeah? What are you going to do? Tell our parents?"

I swallow. "You're all the same, aren't you?" My voice is quieter than I expected, edged with emotion. "Men. Men who hurt women." Like last night, his expression falls for a second. *Good.* I keep pushing. "You rape us," I growl, and his eyebrows fly up. "Defiling us, teasing us, invading our space, ensuring even our *home* doesn't feel safe," I add, my lips trembling slightly.

I stand up taller and look at Ledger. "If you ever touch my things again, I will report you."

My eyes flick to Hunter again, and I swear some sort of mercifulness—understanding—appears on his face.

I twist around and walk back to my locker, my whole body shaking.

A few people clap, but the murmurs soon die down.

People are still terrified of the Kings, but I'm about to pull a checkmate.

Hunter, Ash, Ledger, and Samson are about to witness how this Queen attacks—slow, premeditated, and lethal.

14

SAMSON

Something about her makes me want to protect her from the guys—makes me want her all to myself. Sometimes they go a step too far, and today is one of those days. I know Hunter has mixed feelings because of his mom, but his feelings for Briar are starting to cloud his vision.

I know because I was the exact same way once with Micah.

Thinking of Micah—of *us*—is really fucking hard. I close my eyes briefly and will the memory of the man I used to love—the man who's gone now—out of my mind.

"She likes to play the victim, but secretly she enjoys it," Ash murmurs as we walk through the hallways to our next class. "Did you see the tramp stamp?" he adds, nudging my side.

I nod, shoving my hands in my pockets. "Yeah."

"Slut," he murmurs.

Before I can respond, Hunter shoves Ash against the locker. "Don't call her that," he growls, walking away to his next class.

I look at Ash, displeased. Sometimes his vulgarity gets annoying. None of us are really like that. We may be dicks, but we're not going to go around slut shaming women.

Briar intrigues me, baffles me, surprises me. I can see the strength shining behind her eyes, the tenacity and resoluteness.

You're all the same, aren't you?

Briar is a fucking badass—a survivor.

Why the fuck are we trying to torment her when we should be trying to recruit her?

As Ledger, Ash, and I walk to our next class together, I think about how we became the *Kings* of Ravenwood—a title I *still* don't deserve. Mob mentality is a funny thing, and it just sort of happened after Micah. None of us bothered to correct them—not with who our families were. It was so much easier to fit into the mold everyone had already created for you.

Hunter was the original *King*. His dad being the headmaster meant he was automatically the leader of our class. He's a free spirit, eclectic, and intelligent—when he's not being an ass. In fact, he's my favorite person to talk to. His dad is a world traveler, and they've been to some cool places. People misunderstand him.

Ash came second. As the mayor's son, his position as Hunter's beta formed naturally. He hides behind his vulgarity and comes off as a total dick to most people, but I know the truth. The Greythorn family has more secrets than anyone I know, and Ash bears the brunt of it all as the only child.

And Ledger, the all-star athlete with a future in track and field. He goes against the grain to spite his parents, but it doesn't matter, because despite the piercings, the tattoos, the defiance... he can do no wrong, and his family connections have saved him on numerous occasions. Life comes easy to Ledger Huxley. His *I-walk-on-water* attitude gets on my nerves, but he's loyal as fuck, and a good friend.

And me? I don't quite know where or how I fit in, but Ash befriended me freshman year, and I've been here ever since.

As we sit down in economics, Hunter scans the classroom for Briar, who has this class with us. Again, that overprotectiveness reverberates through my body, and I shove the feeling away.

Just as the second bell rings, Briar slips into the room, glaring at each of us before taking a seat, completely put together and composed.

Badass.

Ledger quirks an eyebrow as he flips his computer open to the virtual textbook, and Ash thumbs his lower lip suggestively as his eyes rove over Briar's legs. Hunter just stares straight ahead with furrowed brows, his arms crossed, trying to ignore her.

She's an enigma, and we all seem to want a piece of her.

15

BRIAR

Scarlett texted me she's convinced that everyone is now just as wary of me as they are of the *Kings* after this most recent showdown, and that I now have my own bad rap as the person dumb enough to defy the Kings. I meant it when I said I wasn't here to deal with this bullshit. I am here to get through the year, to add it to my resume, and to get into the Sorbonne in Paris. I didn't ask for any of this.

Except, maybe I did when I fought back that first day...

I'm still fuming after economics class. I swallow as I walk out of the classroom after the bell rings. I didn't look back at the boys the entire class—which took a lot of self-control. When I walk up to where Scarlett and Jack are already eating lunch, they both whoop and holler as I blush and sit down.

"Oh, please. They need to be taken down a peg," I explain, holding my hands out.

"Yeah, but you just like... stood there all Xena-like, your hair flowing, your bra showing..." Jack trails off, his voice high-pitched and excited. "It's like one big alpha show." He shakes his head and takes a sip of his iced coffee.

I raise my eyebrows. "What's an alpha show?"

"Jack reads a lot of wolf shifter novels," Scarlett explains.

Jack places his palms flat on the table and grins like I just asked his favorite question. "Okay, so every pack has an alpha wolf. Obviously, that's always been Hunter. But then you showed up, and it's like you're trying to get him to kneel *to you*—like you refuse to submit."

"I do refuse to submit," I answer, taking a bite of my sandwich.

Scarlett laughs. "See?" She looks at Jack. "We were so worried when we saw her, but look at how she's holding up." She smiles at me. "I'm proud of you."

I shrug. "Really though, they're just guys. Rich, snobby guys who are used to getting their way. I see right through them."

I don't admit to the fear lurking underneath my courage—the small, nagging feeling that they are still men.

Men who could hurt me.

"It'll be interesting to see who wins," Jack adds, cocking his head. "Truthfully, I just want to see Ash cry," he confesses.

"Why Ash?" I ask, laughing.

Scarlett and Jack look at each other briefly. "As much as we hate him, it's not our story to tell. But let's just say that

Ash and Jack had a thing the summer before freshman year."

"What?" I screech, grinning. "Ash? The douche?"

Jack rolls his shoulders as if he's trying to repel the memory. "We were young, and he wasn't always such a douche."

"Ash broke his heart," Scarlett declares, chewing her salad loudly. "Jack is always looking for ways to get back at him."

I chuckle as I sip my water. "Everyone sleeps with everyone here," I mumble.

"If you ever want to kiss a girl," Scarlett starts, and we all laugh.

"You'll be the first person I proposition," I answer.

Fortunately, the *Kings* give me the space I need to recalibrate, and I don't see them the rest of the day. *Dumb move on their part because this Queen is always thinking one step ahead.* I head home, finish homework, and then spend the rest of the late afternoon watching TV. Mom and I eat dinner together—some pasta recipe she learned from a yoga friend. It's delicious, and I go back for seconds just as Hunter walks into the dining room, grabbing a plate.

Oh, hell no.

"Smells delicious, Aubrey," he purrs. I hate the way he says her name. I hate the way he says everyone's name. Like he loves to hear himself talk.

He's wearing a thin, worn white T-shirt and black jeans that fit his sculpted legs without being too tight. Button-up boots complete the look, and I wonder, as I study his tan forearms, why he has to be so good-looking while also being such an ass. To my chagrin, he sits down right next to me.

"Briar," he says slowly, twirling his pasta. "How lovely to see you."

I narrow my eyes at him. "Hello," I answer, pushing my plate away. I cross my arms, and the gesture exaggerates my cleavage.

Hunter's eyes flick to my chest and then back up to my eyes, slightly darker than they were a second ago. Then he shakes his head and looks away, running a hand through his hair.

"How's school going?" my mom asks, taking a large bite and chewing loudly.

Oh, the innocence. She has no idea what school is like for us.

Her eyes flit between us, and I have to wonder if she suspects there's something more going on. She has that curious, bright look in her eyes, and when she meets my gaze, a knowing smile forms on her lips.

Great.

"I think Briar is fitting in quite well," Hunter muses. Even the way he eats—the way he chews—is perfect, coordinated, elite. He holds his utensils like someone who's used to eating in fine dining establishments.

God, I hate him.

"That's great!" my mom chirps, facing Hunter. "She was worried about Ravenwood being a private preparatory school and all. It's so different from the school she left..."

Hunter's lips twitch as he takes a sip of water. I watch the way his throat bobs, the golden skin there flawless except for the day-old dark stubble. I like how he doesn't shave—just a close trim, leaving a thin, dark layer that gives him an edge. Shaking the thought away, my eyes find his, and he smirks as if he knows I was checking him out.

"I assume that means you've both decided to get along?" she adds, her expression hopeful. She *so badly* wants us to get along—*so badly* wants me to find my place here in Greythorn, and ultimately Ravenwood. A place to shuck my trauma. A fresh start. And I know that getting along with my dear stepbrother is one way to do that.

As I look at Hunter—the way his calloused hands grip the drinking glass roughly, the tips of his fingers white as his eyes find mine again—I know we'll probably never have that. There's too much of something I can't quite put my finger on.

Tension.

Competition.

Aggression.

Abhorrence.

"We have," I answer, giving Hunter a sweet smile. I swear, he's seconds away from shattering the glass in his hands. "And his friends have been nothing but kind to me, too."

Hunter's brows furrow ever so slightly, but before he can respond, Andrew walks into the dining room. He smiles and throws his arms wide, clad in jogging pants and a T-shirt. He bends down and gives my mom a long kiss on the lips. I avert my eyes and focus on the pasta, feeling Hunter's eyes on me.

"Well, well, well," he muses, grinning as he sits. Scooting closer to my mom, he looks at Hunter and me. "Isn't this nice? Sitting down to eat as a family again. I say we make this a weekly thing," he suggests.

My mom nods, grinning. "Or daily! We have all of this

space, and a beautiful room to eat in," she adds, looking at me. "What do you think, Briar?"

I shrug. "Sure," I reply, refusing to look at Hunter.

Annoyance rolls through me as his arm snakes around the back of my chair. "I think it would be wonderful to sit down as a family," he agrees, smiling. Andrew and my mom smile and kiss again, nuzzling noses. They can't hear the bite—the *threat* in Hunter's words.

I slide my eyes to his and narrow them, frowning.

"Don't you think that'd be nice, Briar?" he taunts, leaning back and smiling at me salaciously. His shirt clings to the muscles of his abdomen, not an ounce of fat on him. Just strong, honed muscle everywhere. "Maybe Ash, Ledger, and Samson can join us every now and then," he suggests.

Andrew nods. "We'd love to have them," he says cheerfully. He smiles and helps himself to a heaping pile of pasta. "They're welcome anytime."

I'd rather die.

Hunter chuckles. "I know they'd love that," he quips, his eyes sliding to mine. He winks, and I look away.

I want to slap the cocky smile off his face.

16

Briar

After dinner, I retreat to my room with every intention of flipping through channels on the TV in my delegated area—according to Hunter's house rules. The prick had the audacity to install a flatscreen above my dresser after our argument the other night. The more I think about it, the angrier I get, especially when I try to get comfortable in bed against the hard, wooden frame. A couch would be so much easier.

Why am *I* the one who must sanction myself to my bedroom? I know this was his house first, but there are no posted signs that said the basement was for Hunter Ravenwood's use only. As far as I'm concerned, this is just as much my house as it is his, now that our parents are married, and my mom and I are fully moved in. I have no doubt that our parents would back me up if push came to shove.

Throwing the covers off and climbing out of my bed, I stomp down the hallway and then down the stairs. It's nearly ten, and I know my mind won't let me sleep until I've zoned out for a bit. He might not even be in there. He could be sleeping.

But something tells me the devil doesn't sleep.

I glance into the library for a second as I pass it. I stop abruptly when my eyes adjust to the scene before me. The motion must catch Hunter's eye, because his eyes snap to mine. He's sitting at the desk, a typewriter in front of him, and it looks as though he's writing. A *typewriter.* Who even uses a typewriter anymore? His fingers were flying over the round keys effortlessly until I interrupted him, and now he's leaning back and watching me with irritation, his arms crossed.

"Hello, Briar," he says, my name on his lips somehow sensual and smooth.

"You're a writer?" I ask, because I can't think of what else to say—I'm completely caught off guard.

"I'm not a writer," he starts, sighing. "But I do dabble in writing from time to time, yes."

Can't he ever just speak normally?

I walk into the library and lean against the door. The mood in here is dark, old-school—unlike the rest of the house, which is a bit airier. The shelves lining the paneled-wood walls are stuffed full of books. There's a leather Chesterfield sofa, and the desk where Hunter sits next to the grand window is large and ornate. He's watching me impatiently.

"So, what do you write?" I ask casually.

He pushes out from behind the desk and stands next

to me. My pulse spikes, but I hold myself tall and ready myself for a fight.

There's a gleam in his eyes as he leans against the opposite door frame, inches from me. I back up a step, but he reaches out and tugs me forward by my wrist.

"I don't show anyone my writing," he says, his voice rough. His warm hand wraps all the way around my wrist, holding me still. "What makes you think you're special?"

His words clobber me, and my cheeks heat. I try pulling away from him again, but his grip on my wrist tightens. Not enough to hurt—just enough to show how powerful he is. I start to pull away, instinct telling me to fight back, but something about his expression makes me stay. It's unguarded in a way I've never seen before. The way his eyes lock onto mine, the vulnerability somewhere deep within those dark irises... like I caught him doing the one thing he truly enjoys.

I smirk. "It's just a question, Hunter. Not everyone has an ulterior motive."

"I don't trust you," he says slowly, narrowing his eyes. "You're not like the rest of the girls at Ravenwood. You don't bow to anyone, do you?"

I smile and tilt my head. "Absolutely not."

"Well, then it looks like we're at a stalemate."

"I guess we are," I muse, quirking my lips to the side.

"Don't do that," he commands, his brows furrowed.

"Do what?"

"That thing with your lips." His words cause my heart to pound in my chest, and I blink a few times as I digest them. "Why did you move here, Briar?" he asks, leaning forward just enough for me to get a whiff of the vetiver. I open my mouth to state the obvious, but he puts a finger on my lips. "Not your mom's reason. Yours." He pauses. "What happened to you in California?"

A sudden coldness hits me in my core. "What?"

The lines in his forehead deepen as he studies me, something akin to concern passing over his face.

"Did someone hurt you?" His scowl falters for just a second, and I swallow.

"Why would I ever tell you that? After what you did?" I pull out of his grip. "Just leave me alone," I add, my voice sharp and venomous. I twist around and begin to walk away, but his voice stops me in my tracks.

"I didn't know." He sounds almost... anguished. "I had no idea that you would be like..." he trails off, and I turn to face him.

"Like what?" I whisper.

He sighs, trying to find the words. His hand at his mouth, brushing against his full lips, causes me to stare.

"I expected a little girl. Not you." His eyes narrow ever so slightly, and he pushes me against the door frame. *Should I be worried right now? Because I'm not...* He has hands on both shoulders now, pinning me beneath him. Sighing, I look him straight in the eye as I tell him.

"I was raped. He's in prison. End of story."

His eyes bore into mine—the dark brown irises rich and beautiful. *Cunning.* And yet... they soften as my words plow through him. He releases his grip slightly, licking his lips as a flash of anger crosses his face.

"I'm sorry that happened to you," he growls.

I shrug. "It's in the past now. I'm working through it." Furrowing my brows, I stare at him. "Which is why I might've overreacted to you touching me." Understanding passes over his face. I continue. "I'm still not sure why you felt the need to be mean, anyway," I confess. "I never did anything to you, and yet you humiliated me."

And there it is. One of my most vulnerable thoughts.

"I was annoyed," he starts, the corners of his lips quirking upwards. "I was acting out. The two of you moved in and I sort of lost it," he says slowly. "It's been my dad and I for years. And then you showed up, and I was conflicted. I know it's not an excuse, but at least now you know where my head was at," he adds, smirking.

"Okay, but today—"

"Will not happen again," he growls, pushing against me. I gasp as his body collides with mine. "I made damn sure the guys knew they were not to touch you ever again. And that was before I knew what *actually* happened. I'm sorry, Briar. Truly."

His words cause my body to heat, my knees to weaken. He... he asked them to leave me alone? He's apologizing?

His words awaken some sort of primal beast inside of me—something fervent and impatient, hot, needy... I lick my lips. I don't know what to say to that. He must realize my hesitation because he presses against me again.

"Now that we're at a stalemate, don't you think we should join forces? Combine our efforts?"

I look away, my cheeks flaming. My core is throbbing, and I squeeze my legs together.

"Your friends would never agree to it," I answer. "They love tormenting people."

He chuckles. "Do they? Are you sure?"

I snap my eyes to his. "Yes, they—"

"Have you seen it with your own eyes?"

His words roll through me, and it takes me a minute to digest them. "You're bullies," I state.

"Are we? Or do we just have a reputation?"

I swallow. *What about Micah?*

I'm about to ask when he thrusts into me, his hips rocking into mine, and I have to stifle my moan. Words have escaped me. I close my eyes for a second before opening them and looking into his brown ones.

Only then do I let myself imagine it—sharing a reign with them. Being *friends* with them—with all of them. Trusting men again—allowing Hunter's protection to shield me, to help me. And then my mind wanders, and I imagine *being* with each of them. Shared among Hunter—the powerful alpha—and Ash, Ledger, and Samson, who all get pieces of me in different ways. The thought causes the space between my legs to throb, causes my throat to constrict. His hooded eyes drink me in, his smile lopsided, like he knows what I'm thinking.

I pull away, trying to forget the ridiculous thoughts running through my mind. Just because he's being *sort of* nice to me, doesn't mean I should be imagining what it would be like to sleep with all of them. It's just so easy to imagine—they're so close, always together... like they come as a packaged deal. I squeeze my eyes shut briefly before taking a step away.

This is a game.

This is all just a game to him.

Another move on the chessboard.

"This is silly. The only thing we need to do is to make a truce. Stop bullying me, and maybe we can be cordial."

"Cordial?" he mocks, a feline smile on his face. He takes a step forward. "Don't you feel it?" he asks, his face not even an inch away from mine. His breath is on my lips, the sweet scent of it turning my core to liquid. He cocks his head and scans my face, the angled jaw defined in the low light of the room. "This thing, between us?"

"Your mom married my dad—"

"So?" he asks, reaching out and running a finger along my jaw.

"So? Even if I did feel it, which I don't, we couldn't."

He smirks, licking his lips. His tongue is long, elegant. I squirm beneath him.

"We don't share blood, Briar. We are not a true brother and sister."

"Still—"

"Why are you fighting it?" he asks softly. "Think about how good we could be. Together." I fight the urge to nod, to agree wholeheartedly, but my mind is screaming at me. "Truth be told, I haven't been able to concentrate since you arrived in Greythorn."

My body heats, and I wonder where my mother is— where Andrew is... and what they'd think if they walked in right now and saw us like this.

"That's your problem," I start, feeling my resolve crumble. "Not mine."

I can't tell if he's playing me—if this is all just one, big prank. But then he pushes me gently against the door frame again, thrusting against me—*God, I wish he'd stop doing that*—and I realize he's not playing. He's very, very serious, and it's evident by the way he presses his thick erection against my stomach.

"Admit it," he whispers, his mouth an inch from mine. My eyelids flutter closed, and my hands press firmly against his hard chest. My nipples peak beneath the t-shirt I'm wearing. As if Hunter can sense it, he lowers his gaze to my chest, and his dark eyes come back up to mine. His dilated pupils are anything but playful—they're enigmatic, ruthless, animalistic. He lowers a hand from next to my head and twists my nipple firmly between his thumb and forefinger.

I cry out, arching my back. I can't help it—it feels *so* good.

That fact surprises me more than anything.

"Or maybe you don't need to. Your body responds to me like a marionette, doing whatever I want it to. Your mind may be fighting it, but your body? It wants me."

I can't even argue with him, can't think of an excuse for the way I'm arching into him and breathing heavily.

"The lion and the lamb," he whispers, sending shivers down my spine as he licks my neck. My pulse thumps against the delicate skin there, and I know he can feel how it's beating erratically. He groans as he devours my skin, and his hips buck against me.

I'm just about to tilt my head up—just about to let him kiss me, and who knows what else, when the front door slams.

We jump apart, and I touch my lips with my fingers.

What the hell just happened?
Did I let him kiss my neck?
Did I feel his hard length against the band of my sweatpants?
Did he confess he's attracted to me?

My head is spinning, and Hunter takes a few steps back just as my mom walks past us, and she smiles as she continues into the kitchen. As if us chatting against a door frame—being *cordial*—is normal. Instinctively, I follow her, and when I look back, Hunter is watching me with a darkened, feral expression, and then he turns back into the library.

"Where did you go?" I ask as I walk into the kitchen, still breathless and slightly dazed.

"Late night Target run. I had this great idea for how to organize the upstairs linen closet."

I nod, and as I begin to turn away, she hands me a chocolate bar.

"Thanks, Mom," I say, my voice catching as I take it. I'm not sure why I'm emotional. The new house, new city, new friends, new problems... It's a lot.

But she's here.

She's always been here.

For that, I will forever be thankful.

"So nice that you and Hunter are hanging out." Her voice is distracted as she pulls clear, plastic bins out of the white bags. Even in jeans and a sweatshirt, she looks so put together. I realize, with horror, that I'm wearing my favorite stained T-shirt. Hunter cornered me and kissed my neck in my schlubby pajamas. I make a mental note to buy some nicer ones.

For *me*, not for him.

"Mmm hmm," I mumble, unsure of how else to respond. "I should go to bed. Night, Mom." I give her a quick peck.

I walk back to the library, and Hunter's eyebrows rise with amusement as he watches me walk toward him. I set the candy bar down and slide it to him.

"A peace offering," I explain, giving him a small smile.

Before he can respond, I walk out and to my room, closing the door and trying to calm my racing heart.

17

Ledger

I bend down and tie my sneakers, looking up just as Briar comes onto the track. I stifle a laugh as she glowers at everyone, her expression sour and displeased.

My dark, little rain cloud.

I jog over to her.

"Listen," I start, putting my hands on my hips. "I'm sorry about yesterday."

She glares up at me. "I honestly don't care."

I reach out and grab her hand, but she pulls away, as if I've burned her.

"Don't touch me," she hisses.

I hold my hands out. "I'm not going to hurt you, Briar. I'm just trying to apologize."

She scowls, looking down at the track. I've noticed her nose wrinkles whenever she's upset, and I hide my smile because it makes her seem so innocent.

"I don't understand why you continue to taunt me," she starts, looking up at me. Her eyes are wide, open.

"I didn't know," I explain, running a hand through my hair. "None of us knew about..."

"Hunter told you."

Her words are resigned, and I swear I hear a hint of relief, too.

"He said we shouldn't fuck with you anymore." She looks at me and doesn't say anything, though I can tell the wheels are churning. "I'm not a bad guy, Briar. People think I'm this tough jock, but that's their assumption, and I never bothered to correct it."

She looks up at me through her lashes. "Why steal my shirt then?"

I shrug. "I was just teasing you."

"I'm waiting for an apology," she quips.

I smile. "I'm sorry."

"Thank you." She gives me a small smile in return, and then she begins to stretch, lifting her arms over her head. I catch her starting to open and close her mouth a few times, like she wants to say more, but she must decide against it because she bends forward.

I don't mind the view...

"What do your tattoos mean?" she asks suddenly as she snaps up.

I smirk. "That's second date territory, so you'll have to wait and see."

A flush creeps up her neck as my words sink in. "You're so full of shit, do you know that?"

I begin to walk backward, throwing my arms wide and cocking my head. "One day, little lamb."

I'm ready for the chase.

18

BRIAR

For all intents and purposes, Hunter, Ash, Ledger, and Samson all leave me alone the next day at school. I don't know if it's because of what happened yesterday, or my conversation with Ledger during P.E., but there are no more affronts by the Kings. Scarlett is right though—people watch me differently now. The ones who witnessed my shirtless show yesterday must've spread the word that I wasn't going to lie down and take the bullying. A few students look at me with admiration, but also reverence, anticipation... and maybe a bit of fear. I try to smile at everyone I notice glancing in my direction. I want to shout from the rooftops that I'm nothing like them—nothing like the Kings. I am just trying to get through the school year intact, just like the rest of the seniors.

As Scarlett, Jack and I are walking out of the school at the end of the day, Ash saunters up to us. I try not to roll my eyes as we continue to our cars. I suppose Hunter told him to play nice, too.

"Can I help you?" I ask, quirking an eyebrow up.

"Calm your tits, I just want to invite you guys to my party tomorrow night," he says, his voice polite.

"A party? The omnipotent Kings throw parties?" For a second, confusion flashes across his face, but it's gone just as quickly as it appears.

He looks at Jack. "Tell her I always throw parties." I notice the way his eyes linger on Jack for a second too long, and again, something flashes in his expression.

"It's true. We don't usually go, though," Jack answers, crossing his arms. His response says everything I need to know.

Ash sighs and turns to me. "Please come. I promise we don't bite." His eyes flick to Jack. "Except in certain situations."

Jack chokes, covering it with a cough.

"What time?" I ask, crossing my arms.

He grins, his light blue eyes twinkling. If he wasn't such an ass, his smile might make me blush.

"For you, anytime."

"Jackass," Scarlett mumbles. If Ash hears, he doesn't say anything.

"I think we already have plans but thank you." I push past him.

"Hunter really wants you to go," he says, pleading.

Jesus.

First Ledger, and now Ash?

"Hunter can ask me himself, then." I grab Scarlett's and Jack's hands, pulling them behind me as we leave Ash by the gate of the school.

"What was that all about?" Scarlett asks, and we stop in front of my car.

I shrug. "Hunter and I have come to a sort of... ceasefire," I explain, feeling immediately guilty that I didn't tell her or Jack what happened last night. "After everything happened yesterday, he told the guys to leave me alone. I think we're... cordial now?"

"Cordial? With the Kings?" Scarlett quips, her voice hesitant. "They are *jerks*, Briar. They don't know how to be friends with anyone else. Trust me, other people have tried to breach the ironclad wall they have around themselves."

I don't know what to say to that. On the one hand, it's kind of true. But on the other hand, I don't think Hunter acquiring a new stepsister was in their grand plan, so sometimes things change.

"We're both tired of clashing. So, we agreed to a peace offering. We're *not* friends," I clarify. I think about the chocolate bar—about the way my coffee was ready and waiting for me this morning. Sure, it could've been my mom. She was up early for a meeting with a potential client. But something told me it was one of the other occupants of my new home.

"Be careful, Briar," Scarlett warns. "I don't trust them."

I laugh. "*They* shouldn't trust *me*."

I text Sonya—my therapist in California who is paid for 24/7 text access, thanks to my mom—and update her on everything that's happened. She doesn't respond right away, but when she does, her blunt answer surprises me.

You've been through the ringer, Briar. And we've

been working on letting the trauma go, learning how to feel good again. Learning what feels good. I need you to listen to your body, your intuition. After all, one of them is family...

I stare at my phone for a few minutes after reading her text.

One of them is family...

But it's sort of true. After last night, something about Hunter changed. He went from irritated at having to share his space—the space his mother once occupied—to protective of me.

Maybe... maybe they're not as bad as everyone makes them out to be.

I'm in the middle of a shower a few minutes later, just before dinner, when the power goes out. Groaning, I step out and feel for my towel, and then I carefully search for the door handle. I left my phone on my bed, but since it's dark out already, I can't see a damn thing. I finally make my way back into the bedroom when someone pounds on my door.

"Mom?" I ask, turning on the flashlight setting on my phone.

"No," a voice says, and goosebumps rise on my wet skin.

I throw the door open. "Hi?" I pull the towel tighter.

"They went to grab dinner," he says, running his hands through his hair. "Just wanted to make sure you were all right."

Okay, so maybe having a stepbrother isn't so bad.

Ignoring the warm feeling spreading throughout my chest, I tilt my head as water continues to drop onto the carpet. His words from last night enter my mind as his brows knit together ever so slightly with concern.

Are we bullies? Or do we just have a reputation?

"I'm fine," I answer. He nods, and just as he turns to walk away, "Thank you for checking on me."

He gives me a small smile, his eyes rolling over every exposed inch of my body.

"I like your tramp stamp, by the way. I forgot to tell you yesterday."

I blush. "*That* was a drunken, spur-of-the-moment mistake when I was fifteen," I laugh, referencing the Magic 8-Ball on my lower back. "I had a fake ID, got plastered, and then got a tattoo."

He smirks. "Well, it suits you."

As he walks away, I want to ask him to stay—want to see more of *this* side of Hunter Ravenwood. The nice one—the one who comes to check on me.

But I don't.

Because though we're at a stalemate now, I have no idea how long it'll stay that way.

After all, only one alpha wins the final battle.

When the lights come back on a minute later, Hunter walks past my door. I notice his shadow pause for a second, but then he continues to his room without knocking.

One of them is family...

19

BRIAR

"No," I declare, turning to look at myself in my mirror. When I'd convinced Scarlett and Jack to go to Ash's party, I did not expect Scarlett to go full-on makeover mode on me.

"Oh, come on," Scarlett whines. "You look fucking hot."

"Speak for yourself," I murmur, my eyes taking in Scarlett and all her glory.

She opted for a silver, metallic suit with a black tie, and she finished the look off with her platform Docs. Her short, dark hair is slicked back, and her heavy makeup looks amazing.

I glance back at my reflection. A lacey, short, skin-tight dress clings to my body. The arms are see-through, and I feel like a sexy Morticia Addams with my loose waves and red lipstick.

"Please," she begs. "Pretty please?"

Jack makes an annoyed sound from my bed as he scrolls on his phone. He's not really paying attention since he's already dressed in a black shirt, black jeans, and a silver tie that perfectly matches Scarlett's suit.

I look back at myself. For one, my ass is nearly hanging out. Two, this is not really my style. I'm all about function and comfort over style. If I had my way, I'd be wearing my jeans, Converse, and a tank top, but Scarlett seemed completely appalled by that idea.

"You are the Queen of Ravenwood. You need a show-stopping dress. Not some jeans and a tank from American Eagle."

I frown at her. "Fine. But I'm not wearing heels." I instead opt for my Docs, lacing them up as we get ready to head out. I turn to Jack, studying him. "What exactly happened between you and Ash?" I ask. It just seems like such an unlikely pairing. Sweet, sarcastic Jack, with his ginger hair and thick glasses... and Ash. The most overconfident guy at Ravenwood.

He sighs. "We were young and stupid. That's all I'm going to admit."

"Even *I* don't know what really happened," Scarlett muses, walking over to Jack and giving him a soft smile.

Jack frowns. "I really liked him, and he really liked me, but he got scared and pulled away." He shrugs. "It was nearly three years ago."

"So, when Micah started dating Samson," Scarlett starts, her voice uneven, "we knew what they were about. And we tried to warn him."

"But he didn't listen," Jack finishes.

I look between them, swallowing. "I'm sorry Ash broke your heart," I say, tugging my purse over my shoulder.

He gives me a warm smile. "Thanks."

"Anyway, shall we go?" Scarlett asks.

We head out of my room. My mom is sitting on the couch with her computer on her lap. After the three of us came home earlier, I could tell mom was happy I'd found friends so quickly. And she seemed to like Scarlett and Jack.

"Oh, you guys look great!" she exclaims. "Have a good time." She turns to me. "If you drink, *please* call me and I will pick you up, no questions asked." Turning to my friends, she tilts her head. "Same applies to you two."

"Thanks, Mom," I say as I bend down to give her a hug.

"Thanks, Aubrey," Jack and Scarlett echo.

We say goodbye, climbing into my Subaru.

"Your mom is so cool," Scarlett states as I back us out of the driveway.

"Yeah, having a baby at eighteen will do that to you."

We drive in silence to Ash Greythorn's house. I expect another McMansion, being the mayor's house, but as we weave through the forest, I realize I'm in for a surprise.

The Greythorn's house is not large, but it's the sleekest house I've ever seen—angular, modern, with floor-to-ceiling windows. Surrounded by miles of forest, it's small compared to its surroundings and the houses I'm used to seeing around here. I park behind a string of cars, and even though we're technically on time, the house is already bursting with people.

"I like the house," I muse, tucking my phone in my bra

and handing my keys to Scarlett, who agreed to stay sober tonight.

"You wouldn't if you knew the mayor," Jack answers.

I cock my head as we trek through the grass to the front door, which is propped open.

"Is the mayor a jerk or something?" I ask, pushing the heavy door open all the way.

"You could say that," Scarlett answers.

A shiver works down my spine as music blares through the speakers.

"We'll tell you about it another time," Jack shouts. "I'll get us drinks."

Scarlett and I push our way through the mass of bodies writhing to the music. If I thought I would be overdressed, I was wrong. Greythorn—and Ravenwood in particular—once again proves that most of the people who live here have money. The girls are dressed in stylish clothes and spiked heels. They have perfect hair and makeup. It feels like prom, but with shorter dresses. The guys are all dressed sharply, too. *This is nothing like the laid-back California parties I've been to*, I think, as two girls snort a line of coke next to us.

"Welcome to a Greythorn party," Scarlett yells into my ears. "Where the shoes and watches are designer, the consequences are nonexistent, and the expensive drugs are passed around like candy."

I look around, admiring the stylish furniture, the large, built-in bookcases made of dark wood, and how minimally decorated it is. It's clean and mindful. My mom would love the style of this house—especially the dark green velvet sofa. Someone's set up a state-of-the-art stereo system with a live DJ, the music thumping and vibrating through me. Instead of red solo cups, actual champagne flutes and glass tumblers are being used.

"Where is the mayor? I assume he doesn't approve of these parties…"

"He's probably in Boston or New York for the weekend."

I look around. "What about Ash's mom?"

Scarlett swallows. "She doesn't live here. She's in a psychiatric facility."

Yikes.

I want to ask more, but I know it's too loud and crazy right now. I casually glance around for Hunter, Ash, Ledger, and Samson, but I don't see them. Instead, Scarlett and I make our way to the backyard, intercepting Jack on our way. He slides the door open, and several people are standing around, vaping. The backyard is amazing, with fairy lights lining the tree branches, and no fence—so the forest goes on endlessly behind the house. It's gorgeous. A couple of stylish outdoor furniture sets are placed around the pool, which is lit up with a green pool light. We head to an empty bench near the jacuzzi since it's much quieter there. A few people glance in our direction. As we sit, the closest group gets up and leaves, scurrying off quickly.

"See?" Scarlett asks, sipping her soda.

I take a couple sips of my drink, which tastes like Kool-Aid mixed with vodka—heavy on the vodka. I set it down and look around, frowning.

"See what?" I ask, even though I already know what she's going to say.

"They saw you and left. You have *power* now."

Or a reputation.

Jack and Scarlett chuckle, and we chat for a few

minutes until I get up to use the restroom. It's an excuse, of course. After sipping the rest of my drink, I'm starting to feel sexy in my dress, and as people watch me with reverence, I do feel kind of formidable—but in the friendliest way possible. Like I won't take any shit from bullies, but I also have no plans to torment people the way the Kings do.

Mostly, it feels good to know that the Kings have been knocked down a peg.

As I wait in line for the restroom, I try not to act completely distracted as my eyes scan the crowded house. I use the restroom and walk out, heading to the kitchen for another drink. One of the senior guys—Darian—offers to get it for me, but I refuse. I've watched too many Dateline episodes. He's cute—tall, muscular, with dark hair and bronze skin. We chat for a minute or two, mostly about our French class.

As we're talking, my mind keeps going back to the notion that *this* is how high school is supposed to be. See the cute guy from class, have a nice, innocent conversation... maybe make out after a few drinks. No hierarchy, no caste system. Just innocent teenage drama.

But I know that's not my destiny, and as his arm goes around my shoulders casually, my skin begins to tingle, as if someone's watching us—watching *me*.

I'm laughing at one of Darian's jokes when I see them, and my smile drops from my face immediately.

All four of them are watching me from the other side of the kitchen. They're hidden in the shadow, leaning against the wet bar, and each one is dressed in dark jeans and a black hoodie. I can only see their eyes—Hunter's in particular boring into mine with displeasure. I'm just about to excuse myself from Darian when they turn and walk out the front door.

Stunned, I stammer an apology to Darian and set my drink down. They invited *me*. And yet, as soon as they saw me, they left. What gives? The thought stings as I make my way to the front door.

I wanted to make an impression, wanted to show them I could level up. Until this point, I hadn't realized that this dress was for them. I wasn't sure which of them I was trying to impress the most. I just knew I wanted them all to kneel at my feet and apologize for how they treated me —like maybe tonight could've been the turning point, and we could've been civil to each other from here on out.

Shooting Jack and Scarlett a quick text update that I'm with Hunter and to drive my car home—since they have my keys—I throw the door open and look for them. I rub my arms, the cool air beginning to settle in my bones in this skimpy dress. I shake my head and turn around. As my hands touch the door handle, a car horn beeps a few feet away. The brake lights are on, and I recognize the black Range Rover as Hunter's car.

Smiling, I step off the concrete and make my way to the sleek SUV, my heart thumping nervously in my throat.

20

Hunter

Fuck.

Me.

I never thought a dress could undo me, but I was wrong.

So utterly, gravely wrong.

Ash's party got out of control, and because I know Ash, I suggested we leave in favor of a more interesting activity. He doesn't give two shits if people wreck his house, and I don't blame him—his dad is the world's biggest ass. But I didn't want him to do something stupid.

Briar walks toward my car, a smirk on her red-as-sin lips. I watch her in my rearview mirror, my cock instantly hardening as I drink in her long, pale legs, and the way the dress rides up slightly with each step forward. I remember the feel of her skin, the way it tasted like honey. The way my initial hatred turned to lust. The primal, feral need to have her. I adjust my pants just as she climbs into the back with the guys, since the front seat is filled with trash bags of materials for tonight, and the trunk space is nonexistent thanks to the boxes of books I picked up last week—books I probably won't read but will add to the library, nonetheless.

"I assume this means you'll be giving me a ride home," she says, her voice low. It hits me then—this dress, the way her eyes land on mine—it was for me. *For us*. I saw her looking, saw her long neck crane above the crowd, her grey eyes scanning, hoping to land on one of us.

Come out and play, little lamb.

"If you're good," I answer, and when our eyes meet in the rearview mirror, something darkens in her pupils.

I'm not going to be able to think of anything else until I'm inside of her.

Ash's arms slide around her stomach as she sits on his lap, and I smile.

These guys are my best friends. My soulmates. There is no jealousy. As her stepbrother, I don't care who she chooses to be with, if they treat her right. I'm slowly starting to learn that her presence is shaking up everything I once knew, everything I once thought. I find myself thinking about my friends in ways I never did before, *sharing* her, knowing they're happy, knowing they like her just as much as I do.

Seeing her through their eyes is exhilarating, and something savage burns through me when I think about watching her... with them.

We used to be the *Kings* of Ravenwood.

I guess I never realized until Briar Monroe showed up that we needed a *Queen*.

21

BRIAR

Ash's arms linger a little too long on my stomach, his fingers grazing the delicate skin there. When I twist around, I look into his hooded eyes—the light, ice blue of his pupils that are now a deep, denim blue in the darkness of the back seat. My skin heats as his hardness presses against me, and he squirms almost uncomfortably.

"Look what you do to me, little lamb," he murmurs into my neck.

God, why are they all so beautiful?

The vulnerability on his face right now is stunning. The arrogance is gone, and for the first time, I see him as a human being. His sharp jawline, pronounced cheekbones, and short, black hair can make him seem evil—like a thing of the night. But then I remember what Scarlett said about his mom, about the mayor. We both have a past that haunts us, don't we?

I need you to listen to your body, your intuition.

Suddenly, I find myself leaning back against him, and his hand wraps around me again. This time, he claws at my dress, and my body sparks to life for the first time in a long time.

And it feels really fucking good to be wanted like this.

My intuition is screaming *yes*.

"Where are we going?" I ask, trying to ignore the goosebumps erupting along my skin at Ash's touch.

"You'll see," Ledger answers from next to me. His hood is still on, and he's watching me raptly.

I turn to Samson, who gives me a small smile before turning to face the window.

It hits me then—that I'm in a car with four men who don't have a good reputation. Four men that everyone fears, that control the students at Ravenwood with one look, one word. They have no obligation to keep me safe, other than their word, and history has shown me that I can't always trust men at their word. They can do anything they want to me, and they will probably end up getting away with it, thanks to their family statuses.

Maybe they're still messing with me.

Maybe this is all just a game for them.

But... *maybe it's a game I want to play, too.*

Since day one, they've intrigued me. And something tells me they aren't as mean as everyone seems to think they are. In fact, as I look at each of them, including Hunter in the rearview mirror, I can see how they might be misunderstood—their families essentially run Greythorn, and the other students know it.

But they don't care if people hate them—don't care to

correct the assumptions about them. And there's something commendable about that.

I close my eyes and go through the checklist.

Evaluate my surroundings. *In a car with four guys—one of which is my stepbrother.*

Listen to my gut. *They will take care of me.*

Apply common sense. *Scarlett knows I'm with Hunter, and my mom can track my phone.*

I'm okay.

I'm safe.

I swallow as Ash's other arm loops around my waist. We bounce along the dirt driveway in front of the Greythorn property until we get to the road, and I feel slightly guilty for leaving Scarlett and Jack at the party. I pull my phone out and see a text from Scarlett.

For real? Okay… be safe. We'll take good care of the Soob.

I smile at her nickname for my car, promising myself that I will tell her and Jack everything soon.

Hunter turns on some music when we pull up to a stop sign, and I squirm in Ash's lap.

"What's wrong, little lamb?" Ash whispers, his breath hot on my neck. "You're so tense." He grazes a finger down the side of my body and trails it down my leg. I shudder at his touch, and he chuckles. "You have no idea, do you?" he murmurs.

"What?" I ask, my voice rough, gravelly. My eyes flutter as his hand runs back up my leg, and my skin pebbles beneath his touch.

"How much we already possess you, body and mind." The answer sends a shock wave of pleasure through me.

His hand moves to my inner thigh. "Do I make you wet?" he asks, and I close my eyes.

Filthy. He has a filthy mouth, and my body is betraying me by reacting this way.

"You wish," I answer, finding the tiniest bit of resolve.

"Liar," he whispers, his breath fanning out across my neck. "Why are you denying it?"

"I'm not, I just—"

"You wouldn't fight it, would you? If I could make you come so hard that you saw stars?"

I let out a tiny gasp. *Holy fuck.*

"Admit it," he murmurs, his fingers finding my panties. I let my legs part just slightly, granting him access. It's been so long since I've known pleasure like this. And I've never been with a guy—with *guys*—who knew what they were doing, who knew just the right words to make me part my legs for them. It was always sex, sure, but it was awkward and stilted. And this? This feels so damn natural, so good. "Admit that you would scream if I was deep inside of you, fucking you senseless."

Jesus.

His dirty talk doesn't surprise me. I twist around to face him and place an arm around his shoulders. I open my mouth to say something, but his hand moves my panties to the side, and he takes a ragged breath.

"I was right, Briar. You're already soaking wet for me," he mutters, and I see it then—the hunger in his expression—the moment of being a real fucking human. His reputation prevents him from dropping his guard with anyone else but us—anyone else but *me*.

"Who says it's for you?" I ask, my voice low.

He opens his mouth to retort, but instead, he punishes me by slipping a calloused finger into my wet slit.

I arch my back against him, thankful for the music, thankful for the fact that Ledger is looking at his phone, Samson is looking out the window, and Hunter is driving. *Thankful for the darkness.*

"Stop fighting it," he whispers into my ear and pulls me closer. He thrusts his hard cock against my ass, and though I don't hear it, his voice hums in pleasure, his body vibrating with need. I'm about to move his hand when he slips his middle finger into my pussy, his thumb working my clit.

"Let me own you," he growls, nibbling my neck.

"Yes," I whisper, my voice barely audible.

And then he inserts another finger into my pussy. My dress hides what he's doing—it just looks like his hand is between my thighs. Only his fingers curve and flick against the sensitive spot, his thumb pressing down on my clit. There's no outward friction, but whatever he's doing with his fingers, whatever angle he has them in…

I arch my back further, throwing my head back as heat courses through me. I pleasure myself, of course, but this is the first time I've let someone touch me since Cam. I haven't wanted to until now.

We've been working on letting the trauma go, learning how to feel good again. Learning what feels good.

"Good girl," he says, his voice breaking. He's subtly moving his cock against my ass at the same time, and the thought of him coming undone—of Ash Greythorn coming undone because of *me*—sends me over the edge.

I manage to hold myself as still as possible, and when I look up into the rearview mirror, Hunter's dark eyes bore into mine, as if he can sense I'm coming. I grip Ash's forearm tightly as wave upon wave of my climax rips through me, the feeling clawing out from inside and spreading along my limbs in a hot, fiery tempest of pleasure. My eyes never leave Hunter's, and something must pass over my face because he grips the wheel tightly, his fingers white against the firm leather.

"What did I tell you?" Ash asks, removing his hand and licking his fingers. "Wet as a whistle. Did you know that you taste like vanilla ice cream?" he whispers into my neck, gently placing a kiss against the hot skin there.

"Fuck off," I whisper, my voice shaky.

He just chuckles, and when I look back into the rearview mirror, Hunter is watching me with fervor.

22

BRIAR

About five minutes later, we pull up to a large building with a wrought-iron gate guarding the entrance. The gate is open, and Hunter pulls up to the front of the building. It's dark, and obviously not open or inhabited—if the shuttered windows and lack of lighting are any indication. Once we park, Samson opens the door and hops out. I follow, ignoring the way Ash's hand grazes my upper thigh. Hunter and Ledger walk around the car, and Ledger throws his jacket over me. Each guy is holding a flashlight, and Ledger hands one to me.

"Thanks." I give him a small smile. "Where are we?"

"Medford Asylum," Hunter answers. "An abandoned psychiatric hospital. One of the most haunted places in Massachusetts."

My skin breaks out in goosebumps. "Why are we here?" I ask, looking around. A sign hangs precariously over the large gate, and it creaks as it swings in the cool night breeze. "Shouldn't Ash be monitoring the party at his house?"

Ash laughs, and it's not a nice laugh. "I don't give a flying fuck if they burn the place down."

Hunter's eyes scan my bare legs. "Let's go," he commands, handing each of us a backpack filled with what sounds like soda cans, if the heavy clacking of aluminum is any indication.

The five of us walk to the front of the hospital. I follow Hunter, practically on his heels as we climb the short staircase to the front door. Hunter tries the door, and it doesn't budge, so he takes a step back and kicks it open with such force that it startles me. I follow him inside, with Ash, Ledger, and Samson behind me. Our flashlights illuminate a few feet in front of us, but beyond that, it's all black. Thank God for my boots, because the floor is littered with dirt, broken glass, and trash.

"This is so fucked," Ash says, walking ahead of me. I swallow, thinking of his mother and what he must be thinking to be walking through a place like this. He kicks a piece of trash and walks ahead of all of us.

I walk up to Hunter. "Is he okay?" I whisper, stepping over a large pile of dirt. What Scarlett told me earlier—paired with his response to leaving the party...

His father must be a terrible person.

"We all have our demons, right?"

His lips tick upwards ever so slightly. The hardness in his expression—the crease between his brows that usually runs so deep—softens slightly as he watches me. It's not full-blown vulnerability, but it's a small token of friendliness—of camaraderie.

So different from the first few days we knew each other, when it was mean and cruel… it's as if the roles of the Kings were created for them, and they never bothered to correct anyone.

"Yo, check this out," Ledger calls, walking into a room off what must've been the admissions desk. My flashlight illuminates several overturned chairs on the floor, and a large desk under a shattered, protective window sits in front of us.

I turn right and follow Ledger into the mystery room. It's deathly quiet in here, away from the other guys. The moon shines through a large, barred window. I shine my light on the metal wall to my right, and then with a sinking, sick feeling, I see the autopsy table in the middle of the room, the metal dented and scratched with a layer of dust atop it.

"This is wild," I murmur, walking around the table and then up to the body shelves. I pull one open and slide the table out, which makes Ledger jump back.

He chuckles. "This doesn't scare you?"

I shake my head. "Why would it?" *I've seen far, far scarier things in my eighteen years, Ledger Huxley.*

"I just assumed…" He puts his hands in his pockets.

"Does it scare *you*?" I smirk.

He leers down at me, the flashlight giving his face a ghoulish look. "No." He smiles. "The living scare me way more than the dead."

I cock my head. "The living? Like whom?"

He smiles, taking another step closer. "My parents. Their friends." He rolls his eyes. "Religion can do a number on vulnerable people—can turn them into monsters."

"Your parents are religious?" I ask, crossing my arms.

He chuckles. "You could say that."

I look at him—*really* look at him. "But you're not like that," I muse, narrowing my eyes.

"Definitely not," he murmurs, his voice low. "I like fucking, and drinking, and debauchery too much," he growls.

My pulse speeds up as his eyes flit down my body once. I try not to notice the way his tongue moves with the stud, or the way his pouty lips look pillowy and butter soft. His blue eyes find mine again, and his blonde, disheveled hair gives him an unhinged look—especially with the moonlight pouring through the window.

He reaches out and slips the backpack off my back, and it falls to the floor with a loud, metallic thud. A hand curls around the hair at the back of my neck, and I gasp just as his coat—the one over my shoulders—falls to the floor.

"You're not like the other girls, Briar. You give zero fucks, and you're the only person who's not afraid of us." He bends down, his breath on my cheek. Pressing his hard body against my back. "I thought you'd run away screaming by now, but here you are."

"You don't scare me. None of you do."

With his hand fisted around my hair, he yanks me backward ever so slightly, his mouth near my ear. "Is that why you let Ash finger fuck you in the car just now?"

His words turn my core molten, and I inhale sharply. "So what? Are you jealous?"

He laughs, the sound dark and unhinged. "What do you want, Briar?"

"You tell me," I say, trying to pull out of his grip, but he just tightens his hold. "You're all so hot and cold. I can never tell if you... if you want me, or if you're messing with me."

He pulls me backward again, and this time the entire back of my body collides with the front of his—including the bulge in his pants.

"I think you have your answer, yes?"

I inhale sharply. "Yes," I whisper. "But—"

"Do you want me?" he asks, fingering my hair. I moan in response, his touch causing a spark of pleasure to work its way down my neck and spine. "Good. Have you thought about how it would feel to fuck each of us? To see how we're all different..." One hand reaches around, grazing my taut nipples beneath the fabric of the dress. "Or perhaps how we're the same?"

Breathless, I shake my head. "I haven't thought about it."

He chuckles. "You're such a fucking liar, little lamb. Are you trying to convince me that you're not wet for me, too? Minutes after Ash fucked you with his fingers?"

I gasp again as he grinds into me. "I'm not—"

"Let me ask you again. Does your pussy get wet whenever I pull your hair?" He tightens his grip on my strands, making my scalp sting and tingle in the best way possible.

Pain and pleasure.

"You wish," I growl, my voice fractured. But despite my best efforts to resist, I push my ass against him, wanting more.

His mouth is on my neck as he whispers, "Maybe I should check."

I clench my legs together, and he must know, must assume I'm bursting for his touch, because he trails a hand down to my legs and lifts my dress up to my waist. I arch into him, waiting...

"What the hell is going on?"

Ledger and I jump, and a second later, my stepbrother comes into view, his dark eyes finding mine. His expression is veiled and unreadable—and he looks down at my dress gathered at my waist. When his eyes snap back to mine, his expression is lecherous, with a lopsided smile forming on his lips.

"Seems as though my sister can't get enough of my friends," he says slowly, circling us. "First Ash, now Ledger... Should I call Samson now, or will you wait to fuck him on the drive home?"

"Maybe she wants all of us at once," Ledger teases, his voice dark.

The words heat me from the inside out, and even though the thought of being with all of them intrigues me, I pull away from Ledger's grip and pull my dress down. I grab Ledger's jacket and my backpack. Hunter's eyes don't leave mine the entire time, but he doesn't answer Ledger, doesn't acknowledge what happened between us in the library at home last night. The notion stings a bit—that maybe he doesn't want me after all of that. Embarrassment floods through me.

"I didn't realize it was a crime to enjoy casual sex," I answer, glaring at Hunter.

"It's certainly *not* a crime. You may enjoy as much dick as you want," he adds, his face hard. "But maybe try not to fuck all of my friends in one night."

Ledger laughs. "Sounds like someone's jealous of his sister's sexual exploits."

Hunter runs a hand through his dark hair. "I promise you, I'm not."

And then he turns and walks out, leaving me stunned.

For some reason, his rejection erases the experiences with Ash and Ledger. I am getting carried away, falling for their titles and their power, opening my legs for them...

And the one I want the most doesn't want me back.

23

Ash

I'm still high as a kite from the smell of Briar's pussy—which is saying a lot, because I was in a pretty messed up place when we left my house. Something about watching other people destroy my dad's house spurs me on, causes the adrenaline to pump. Hunter noticed, and now, here we are—even though we weren't supposed to fuck Medford up for a few more weeks. I smile and pull my fingers to my nose, inhaling the sweet smell. Hunter catches me once or twice, giving me an annoyed look. Technically, I finger fucked his sister.

And I know it bothers him that he wasn't the first to do it.

Briar and Ledger walk out of one of the front rooms, and I attempt to hide my smile. I don't blame her for wanting to fuck all of us. I've never been one for polyamory, but I don't think any of us are willing to give her up, so it may just be where we're all headed. I mean, we're closer than most blood brothers. I'd be more worried if she *didn't* want to fuck all of us. I can appreciate the sexual appeal of my best friends. Hunter's bewildering energy, the frenetic, artistic passion that he exudes. Ledger's bad boy vibes—he may look like the meanest one, but deep down, he has a heart of gold, and I know for a fact that a tongue stud can be life changing in bed. And Samson...

I clench my fists as I watch Samson Hall walk ahead of me, careful not to step on the trash littering the floor. He's a smartass—and because of our history, I have a soft spot for him. I shake my head and look away.

It was a long time ago.

"So, are we ready?" Ledger asks, throwing an arm around me.

I nod. "Fuck yes, we're ready." I quickly glance around for cameras. I wouldn't put it past my father to install cameras in a place like this, but luckily, I don't see any.

Samson walks up to me, shrugging his backpack off. He unzips it and holds it out.

"You go first, Ash," he says, his face serious and solemn. Out of all of them, he understands the most—knows the most. He's seen the most—every morbid detail. The others have a vague idea, but I gave Samson the full truth.

I reach in and grab a can of spray paint. "Which room should I do first?" I ask, looking at my friends. I feel oddly nervous, my hands shaking slightly when I pull the cap off.

"What are we doing?" Briar asks, looking around.

"Sending a message to my father," I sneer. "A loud one."

She must've heard about what happened to my mom,

because some sort of understanding passes across her face. Without another word, she grabs a can and then cocks her head, smiling.

"Let's fuck some shit up," she says, using the words I uttered at the burning house a few days ago. My eyes find hers, and my throat bobs.

The guys reach into the backpack and grab a can, and the four of them wait for me to take the lead.

"The more destruction, the better," I snarl, gripping the aluminum tightly. And then I turn, walking into the depths of the asylum—a place that will surely strike a chord with my father once he sees what we're going to do to this place.

24

BRIAR

Hunter drops Ash back at his house around midnight, and the party is still going strong. I'm sleepy, my head lolling against the passenger seat. I'm glad the front seat was empty when we got back to Hunter's car, since we'd used up all the cans. It saved me from deciding which lap to sit on, and Hunter's words still eat at me. I didn't expect to enjoy being with Ash like that—or Ledger.

On the same night.

Still, it's not a crime. Sonya was right. I need to start... exploring what feels good. And truthfully, these last couple of days, being with the guys feels good. Maybe it's because I'm starting to get to know Hunter more, and I know he'll look out for me, but the other guys haven't done anything to lose my trust since the shirt incident.

Since I let it slip about what happened in California.

And I appreciate that they never asked questions—that they knew to stop heckling me.

Because there was once a man who didn't know how to stop.

They make me feel... *alive. Worthy. Sexy.*

And I won't apologize for that.

The guys are still on an adrenaline high as we pull back into the main part of Greythorn. To say we fucked Medford Asylum up would be an understatement. The outside is nearly unrecognizable, and Ash's hope is that it will call for a special election that ousts his father from mayorship. Since Medford is still within the city limits of Greythorn, the news will spread quickly.

I didn't get the full story, but between the bits and pieces Scarlett and Jack told me, as well as the things the guys wrote on the walls... Mayor Greythorn, who's been mayor for twenty years, deserves to go to prison—both for what he did to Ash, and what he did to Ash's mother. Apparently, Christopher Greythorn committed his wife to a psychiatric hospital. Because of his status, she's locked away with around-the-clock security.

Because of him and his lies, she's wasting away in a padded room.

I shake my head. I can't imagine being in a prison like that—unable to leave or go home.

Or see her child.

Ash is stuck living with a monster, so I don't blame him for throwing parties that trash the house—or vandalizing something so personal and metaphorical for Christopher.

I'm starting to realize that the Kings don't cause destruction for no reason.

They cause destruction to get *revenge*.

Samson gets dropped off next, and though I don't know his story at all, I can tell he also comes from money, because his house is just as ornate as the rest of them.

"His parents are doctors, and surprisingly normal," Hunter muses. Ledger makes a sound of affirmation from behind me.

"That explains a lot," I joke.

We drop Ledger off next. He lives in a gated house—like ours. When he closes the door and gestures goodbye, winking at me, Hunter sighs.

"He's old money—related to the writer Aldous Huxley. The Huxley's have lived in the Boston area since before America was founded," he says casually. "His parents are religious and super freaky. They have a wall of crosses and a chapel in their house, if that tells you anything."

I shudder. "That *also* explains a lot," I quip, referring to the piercing and tattoos. We both laugh. "What about you?" I ask, my curiosity piqued. "Are you and Andrew old money?"

He thumbs his lip as we stop at a light. His face is illuminated in red, and he turns to face me.

"My mom was. Some branch of a Brahmin."

I wrinkle my nose. "Brahmin?"

"Descended from pilgrims, similar to Ledger," he muses, and his lips twitch upward. "You really don't know the name Brahmin? It's everywhere in Boston."

I shrug. "California girl." I look out the window, wondering what kind of power trip I've gotten myself mixed up in. These guys aren't your ordinary popular guys—the notoriety goes back generations. These families have been established for *centuries*. I wonder if that's one of the reasons people fear them.

Perhaps the fear, the *reputation* they all have goes back generations—Hunter and the Brahmins. Ledger and the Huxley's. Ash and the Greythorn's...

"Do you like them?" Hunter asks, changing the subject. His voice is gruff, strained.

"Who?" I ask.

"Ash and Ledger."

I let out an exhausted, soft laugh. "No. I mean, maybe? I don't know, Hunter. I like sex. Well, I did." I pause, closing my eyes. "My therapist is helping me to enjoy it again, to listen to my body." I shake the memories of Cam and California away. "So, while it may have seemed like I was whoring it up tonight, it was really nice to just... have fun."

Hunter's throat bobs as he rests his hand under his chin. The gesture makes him seem older, more distinguished—and more arrogant that he already is, if that's even possible.

"I understand, Briar. I'm not jealous, if that's what you think."

I look away and watch as we pass one McMansion after the other. "Okay. It just seemed like you were mad earlier—"

"Mad?" He laughs. "You thought I was *mad?*"

I shrug and turn to face him. "Yeah. When you walked in on Ledger and me, you were acting angry. Like you didn't want your friends to..." *To what?* Touch me? I mean, yes. Ash did pull an orgasm out of me, but in that dark back seat, against his hard on, knowing how *filthy* he was, how daring with his friends surrounding us—I got turned on. But I didn't do that much. It wasn't like I'd fucked all of them tonight.

Once again, the thought of that scenario pierces through me, and I have to bite my lower lip so hard that it nearly bleeds.

"I don't care who you *fuck*, Briar. Fuck one of us, fuck all of us, it doesn't matter to me."

And you? I want to ask. He seems to sense the question on the tip of my tongue.

"You turned me the fuck on. Watching you in the back seat, knowing Ash was being his normal, charming self and probably messing around with you, and then when you looked at me in the rearview mirror..." He parks in our driveway, cutting the ignition. "In the mortuary with Ledger, your ass was pressed into his cock, and you looked so... *happy*..."

I wring my hands and swallow nervously, my face hot. I can't look at him—can't see how his face will be illuminated by the motion sensor near the front door, how his eyes will look darker somehow, like they did last night.

"I'm not blind. I can see how beautiful you are, how defiant you are, how *strong* you are." He pauses. "I want you, Briar." His words are a growl—a confession. Whatever game we started earlier this week is turning very real, very quickly.

I look down, playing with the two rings on my fingers. "We probably shouldn't. If my mom or your dad found out—"

"What do *you* want, Briar?" he asks, his voice edged with something... emotional? I can't really decipher his tone.

I look up then, breaking the spell. And the expression

on his face is that of someone being deprived of a meal after starving. He licks his lips and leans back, spreading his legs.

"Fuck me," he murmurs, narrowing his eyes. His low voice lands in my core, sinking like molten lava. "I dare you. And I want to be the first." He pauses. "You want it, too."

I shift, squeezing my legs together, trying to dispel the throbbing arousal between my legs.

"When did you get so conceited?" I huff and look away. He infuriates me sometimes, but something about him makes me want to rip his clothes off.

A warm, calloused hand lands on my thigh, and it makes me jump. "Take your dress off, Briar."

I wonder if these are lines he practices—if he often sleeps with other girls. I've only been at Ravenwood Academy for a week, so I'm unsure if he or the other Kings sleep around a lot. For all I know, I'm one of many.

The thought should repulse me. I hated guys like him at my last school. The ones who thought they walked on water. I was always immune, always able to pry myself away from their cocky attitudes while every other girl kneeled for them.

But Hunter is different.

Hunter isn't like those high school boys.

As he watches me with amusement, his eyes hooded, I realize he's *nothing* like them. They were boys. They had no worldly experience, no passion, no personality. But Hunter? He's traveled the world. He's a tortured writer. He's witty, and arrogant as all get out because he knows all of this about himself. He's been through some shit—they all have.

Maybe that's why I feel some sort of connection to them.

Because we're not all normal seniors. We all have stories, and pasts, and demons.

We all have our demons, right?

"Do I have to ask twice?" he says, tilting his head and frowning.

I let out a surprised laugh. "You're ruthless."

He just smiles and watches me as I lift the tight, lace dress over my head, practically peeling it off my arms. Then I lean back and smile, crossing my arms as I kick my boots off.

"Move your arms and let me see you," he says slowly, leaning forward ever so slightly.

What are you doing, Briar? He's your stepbrother...

I move my arms and my body heats under his gaze. His expression is serious. Gone is the pompous prick. In his place is an artist studying a piece of art. His jaw ticks as his eyes drink me in. I feel exposed even though I'm in a high-waisted lingerie set with a matching bra. It's my *one* nice pair of undies—and I wore it for them.

He reaches out and moves my hair off my shoulder, exposing my bare neck, my chest. His eyes grow dark, his expression hardening into something wild.

"Get over here," he commands, his voice husky.

I climb over the center console, placing my knees on either side of the seat so that I'm straddling him. I've never been this close to him—not even the other night—and his warm hands pull me impossibly closer.

"Fuck, Briar," he whispers hoarsely. His hand trails over my thigh to the top of my underwear. Following the seam, he moves it to the side, exposing my pussy. "You're soaked," he adds. "I'm not sure if it's from me or from my friends, but both scenarios turn me the fuck on, and my cock might explode soon if I don't fill you to the brim."

I gasp, panting. "All of you make me wet as fuck," I whisper, throwing my head back. "But you..."

He groans and thrusts up into me. I rock my hips against his pants, his rock hard shaft hitting me perfectly. I'm just about to ask him to unzip when he pulls at my panties and rips the delicate lace off of me in one swift motion.

"Hey!" I cry, my voice shrill. "That was my favorite pair."

He laughs, casting them off somewhere behind him. "I'll buy you new ones." *Stupid, fucking rich boy.* His hand trails to my pussy again, and he brushes my landing strip. "I really love this," he rasps, moving his hand down and inserting two fingers with zero fanfare. I gasp, my body exploding into a fiery tempest. His fingers perform a flurry of curved movements that perfectly hit the right spot.

"Fuck," I cry, rocking against him, my body shaking already. He unzips his pants and pulls them down slightly. I barely notice when he reaches up and unclasps my bra, letting the purple material fall to the floor.

"And these are fucking perfect," Hunter whispers, and I look down just as he takes one of my nipples into his mouth, sucking.

"Oh, fuck," I cry, shamelessly riding his hand now. His fingers are still curved inside of me, still doing some sort of dance I've never experienced before—sort of like a light fluttering. Just enough to keep me going, but not enough to push me over the edge.

Teasing me.

"Tell me you want my cock," he says roughly. I can tell he's aroused by the cadence of his voice—uneven and breathless.

"I want your cock inside of me," I beg, all dignity lost.

"Why?" he asks as his length nudges my opening, the skin warm and wet from pre-cum.

"I want to feel you explode," I confess.

"Are you clean?" he asks, kissing my other nipple gently and removing his fingers.

"Yes. And I have an IUD," I answer impatiently.

He purrs. "Good." He pushes against me, his head thick. It stings slightly, because of his size. "Now," he hisses, thrusting upwards in one single motion, claiming me as he enters me to the hilt.

I break against him, bucking my hips and holding onto his shoulders as he slams into me again. A moan rips through me, and one of his hands comes around to the back of my neck, grabbing a handful of hair. The other hand moves my hips against him, directs me, controlling the tempo. The sound of our wetness permeates the air, and the *wrongness* of it all, the fact that we're parked in front of our house, spurs me on further.

He grabs the flesh at my hips and moves me quickly, sliding me back and forth against his rock-hard cock. When he's satisfied with the tempo, he moves a thumb to my clit, pressing down and using his pre-cum as lubricant as he works me slowly at first, but then it gets rougher, quicker, grittier. He strums faster as he gets closer.

I bare my teeth as my climax begins, the dizzying pleasure pulsing through me. My pussy grips his cock, milking him, feeling the way he inhales sharply as his own orgasm starts because of it, finding his eyes as it rips through him like a hurricane, too. I grip his arm, nearly drawing blood, and we both cry out in unison—but I don't close my eyes.

I can't miss it.

I can't miss Hunter Ravenwood coming undone at the seams.

For me.

We're both convulsing as the last of it leaves our bodies, our skin slick with sweat, the windows fogged up, breathing heavily... I collapse against him, my breathing heavy.

He slowly slides out and reaches over to the glove compartment, grabbing a handkerchief.

I look at him skeptically. "Because why wouldn't you have a cleanup rag in your car?" I ask, raising my eyebrows.

He cleans me up without answering, but his mirthful smile tells me everything I need to know. I'm just about to climb back to my seat when his arm holds me to his lap.

"Tonight changed everything," he murmurs. "You're ours now. You realize that, right?"

I laugh. "You can't stake ownership over me."

"I don't mean we own you like a slave," he muses. "But at least for me, now that I've had a taste of you, I don't think I can go back. And I think I can speak for all of my friends."

I pull out of his grip and climb back to my seat, quickly throwing my dress on before opening the door, sliding out, and slamming it shut. When I glance back at him a few feet from the front door, he's watching me with a triumphant smile.

He may think he won—he may think the war is over, that this Queen will bow down to him and the others like all the other students do.

But it's only just begun because I bow to no one.

25

SAMSON

I am just finishing up breakfast when my mom gasps, her eyes on her phone.

"Oh my god, Paul, look at this." She hands the phone to my dad, who scowls at her large screen.

"Who would do such a thing?" he asks, shaking his head.

"What happened?" I ask innocently, my voice feigned with indifference.

Of course I know what happened, because I did it.

"Medford Asylum was vandalized," my mother answers, her voice fraught with displeasure. She clucks her tongue once. "Kathy just texted me, and she heard from Christopher. The things these thugs wrote..." she trails off. "He was only doing what was best for Hannah. That poor woman needed help, and the park incident—"

"How did they vandalize it?" I interrupt, changing the

subject. I don't need a recounting of Hannah Greythorn's mental breakdown. It felt way too close to home.

My mom and dad debate whether they should show me the pictures. In the end, my dad nods, handing me the phone gently, as if that'll help buffer the words on the screen. Someone took the pictures—one of Christopher's employees, or maybe the devil himself.

The words are splashed against the grey stone, haphazard and uneven, large and obvious. We covered most of the front, and a lot of the rooms. I think we all felt like we were avenging our friend and everything he'd gone through. My eyes scan the words—the words we all wrote.

Christopher Greythorn is a monster.

Fuck Chris Greythorn.

Free Hannah.

Greythorn has its own Blanche Monnier.

That last one was my creation. Blanche Monnier was a woman who was locked up for twenty-five years in France in the late 1800s. Her mother, an aristocrat, kept her in one of the many rooms of their manor.

She hadn't seen sunlight for twenty-five years.

Hannah hadn't seen it in five.

Despite her mental illness, Hannah didn't deserve the life her husband sanctioned her to, locked away like a menace to society.

Christopher was the real menace to Greythorn.

"That's awful," I say, eating my eggs and toast in silence for the rest of the meal.

It's truly difficult to conceal my smile.

26

Briar

I spend most of Saturday morning in bed, regretting my actions and anticipating seeing Ash, Ledger, and Hunter next. Would it be awkward in the light of day? Does last night mean I'm one of them—that we're friends? I don't know if we are still competing, or if fucking Hunter's brains out counts as a ceasefire.

Around noon, I finally throw my covers off and shower, taking my time as I shave my legs and wash the smell of *three* guys off me. I don't feel ashamed, exactly—but society is so adamant about choosing one love interest, and the truth is, they all interest me in different ways. I am young—we all are—and I crave adventure. Plus, like Sonya suggested, I need to start exploring what feels good, what feels *right*. It's important to follow my gut, and my gut wants to see where this will lead me.

Everyone is gone as I make a late breakfast. Hunter's

car isn't in the driveway, and my mom had texted earlier that she and Andrew were out picking up some furniture. I shoot a quick text to Scarlett and Jack, and when they respond a few minutes later asking for deets about why I left early last night, I just send the nauseous emoji, hoping that'll explain my abrupt departure. It's not something I want to confess via text.

I catch myself smiling as I make my eggs. I haven't felt this happy in... months. Not since California, not since before Cam and everything that happened.

Shivers crawl down my spine as I think about that afternoon—how I ran away so fearful, so angry. How I knew my life would never be the same, because of one man —and I was right.

I remember how the officers asked me about what happened.

And I told them.

About the rape.

About the knife, and the blood.

About *everything*.

And I knew, in that moment, that I would never be the same.

༺༻

I'm watching TV in the basement an hour later when the doorbell rings. Or rather, an alert pops up on my phone, since Andrew set up the smart doorbell for me. I look down and see Samson on my screen. Hopping up, I climb the stairs and walk to the front door, throwing it open.

"Hey," Samson says, waving.

"Hi," I answer. I cross my arms since I'm not wearing a bra. "Hunter isn't here."

"That's okay. You were with us, so you should know." He gives me a crooked smile that makes my heart flutter a bit. "A reporter is digging into Hannah's story. Someone leaked some photos of what happened last night, and people are beginning to ask questions."

I raise my eyebrows. "Someone?"

He just gives me a small, knowing smile. Something flutters in my abdomen at that look—at the way his eyes find mine, the way his chiseled jaw holds a smirk.

"Here, come in." I step aside so he can enter. "I'll get you a drink."

"Okay, thanks."

We walk into the kitchen, and I move around, trying to find where my mom put the drinking glasses. I find them after opening and closing nearly every cabinet.

"Is water okay?" I ask, setting a glass in front of him. "My mom also has soda, juice, milk..." I look around. "I can find some wine or beer?"

He laughs. "I'm fine with water."

I pour us both a glass of water and sit next to him at the breakfast bar. "Will they release Hannah if they find Christopher at fault?"

Samson shrugs, playing with his glass. I study his profile as he does—his handsome, strong face. The square glasses that perfectly frame his strong brow bones and aquiline nose. His lips are cherry red, making him look sultry and beautiful. And his body? It's strong, large—muscles cut from stone underneath his black shirt and fitted, dark green pants.

"I have no idea, but people are talking, so that's always

a good thing." I'm quiet as I think about Ash—about everything he's endured. Samson continues.

"Christopher is abusive—he always has been," he starts, grimacing, as if it pains Samson to talk about. "I remember freshman year, seeing the bruises..." He looks away. "My whole life, people suspected something was off with the Greythorn's, but no one was willing to do anything about it. When Ash was thirteen, his mother had sort of a breakdown and started wandering around town in her nightdress. She suffered from postpartum psychosis and PTSD. Christopher involuntarily committed her to a psychiatric hospital, and she's been there ever since."

"Jesus. Postpartum psychosis?" I ask.

"She had a late-term miscarriage a few months prior."

My heart sinks. "That's horrible."

"Rumor has it that it wasn't Christopher's."

I swallow. "Wow." When I look at Samson, he's watching me with a funny expression. "What?"

He shakes his head and narrows his eyes. "Are you and Ash an item now?"

I scowl. "No. Did he tell you we were?"

"Not exactly. I was just wondering because of what happened in the car."

I thought we'd been so slick.

"No one has claimed me," I joke, taking a sip of water. "If that's what you mean."

Not exactly.

He angles his head and smiles, his light brown eyes playful and amused. I can't help but smile when Samson smiles. I can tell he has a good soul. He's young and impressionable, like we all are, but one day, Samson Hall is going to rule the fucking world with his charm.

"Would you go on a date with me, then?" he asks.

I rear my head back in shock. "A date?" I ask, shifting in my seat.

He shrugs. "Why not? How about tonight?"

I pull my lower lip between my teeth. "Sure. But you should know that Hunter and I…"

Understanding registers on his face.

"I'm just asking you on a date," he answers, giving me a wicked smile. "I'm not asking you to marry me."

I twist my lips to the side, thinking it over for a few seconds. "Okay. Doe seven work?"

He helps me up as we stand. When his hand touches mine, an electric current zaps down my arm, and he must notice too, because he smiles and kisses my hand. My eyes flutter closed at the contact.

"Perfect. I'll pick you up. Goodbye, Briar." He walks out of the kitchen.

I'm still blushing when the front door closes behind him, and I can't help but smile. They're all so different—and they all bring something different out in *me*. It would be impossible to find a guy with all their good traits—mysterious, filthy talker, bad boy, romantic—and I feel lucky that I get to see what it's like with each of them.

27

LEDGER

I take a quick jog around the perimeter of Greythorn Park, my legs moving me quickly and perfectly on track to beat my record five minute, fifteen second mile time. It's fucking cold out for September. I'm immersed in one of the songs on my playlist, so I don't see them immediately —Briar and Samson.

I slow, watching as they're escorted into *Enclave,* the nicest restaurant in Greythorn. Watching as Samson's hand lightly brushes the back of her red dress and *fuck me* if she doesn't look gorgeous. I continue running, adrenaline coursing through me. I've never felt this rattled by a woman—never this off-kilter. From the moment I saw her, I couldn't focus, couldn't think straight.

And last night? Feeling the way she wanted me, the way her ass rubbed against my cock…

I stop and bend over, pretending to catch my breath. I

run twelve miles on the weekends—I don't ever need to catch my breath. But I do need to hide my growing erection from the people walking around town.

Jesus.

What the hell is wrong with me?

I'm not religious, but she makes me want to kneel before an altar and confess the downright filthy things that run through my mind when I think of her.

I quickly make my way back home, saying a quick hello to Gloria, our house cleaner, before climbing the marble stairs two at a time. Once inside my room, I rip my clothes off and lean against the door, grabbing my throbbing cock and spreading my legs. I bend over myself, stroking fast, hard—*quick and dirty*.

I moan, imagining those red lips from last night around my cock, imagining myself thrusting into her throat, claiming her... My cock twitches in my hand, and I growl, stroking faster, needing release as soon as possible.

My legs begin to shake as I imagine how wet she was for me, how her breathing quickened when I moved her dress up over her waist. Imagine how it would feel to bend her over that table and fuck her brains out.

"Fuck," I rasp, my climax close.

I think about how her skin smelled like honey, how soft and pale she was, how she'd look underneath me as I'd squeeze her large breasts, filling her to the brim with my come...

I cry out as my orgasm rips through me, the pleasure coursing down my legs, more intense than it's ever been. Trembling, I stroke my cock slowly, continuing to pour out onto my floor.

"Fuck," I whisper, closing my eyes.

It takes me a few minutes to be able to even walk to the bathroom to clean up. And as I stare at my reflection —the long, blonde hair, the tongue stud glinting every time I smile, the tattoos on my bare, tanned chest—I imagine how we'd look together.

And it's then that I realize, I'll do anything for just a piece of her.

Even if I must share.

28

BRIAR

Samson takes us to one of the restaurants on the perimeter of the park, and as I glance down at my table setting, I realize this place must be fancy, since there are not two, but *three* forks.

"Shall I order us some wine?" he asks, the corners of his lips tilting upwards, like he has a secret.

"How?" I laugh, resting my elbows on the table and leaning forward. The dress I'm wearing is new—red, silk, form-fitting. I feel like Jessica Rabbit.

He shrugs, his smile real and infectious. "I can make it happen. My uncle owns this place."

I quirk an eyebrow. "I'll have a glass of whatever you're having."

Before I can even ask him about this place—about his uncle, or anything about his life—the server is upon us, and we are showered with not only champagne, but a breadbasket, appetizers, and a salad. It's a flurry of motion that makes me dizzy, and since I haven't eaten in a few hours, I'm ravenous.

"Oh my god," I mumble, my mouth full of delicious, oil-soaked focaccia.

"It's good, right?" He bites off a piece and chews, and we both laugh.

This is so *fun*. With the other guys, it feels sort of... melodramatic. *Angsty*. But with Samson, I kind of feel like a normal eighteen-year-old. Samson orders us dinner, making sure I don't have any allergies, and I let him take the lead. He knows the menu and the food better than I do.

"So, your uncle owns this place?" I ask, sipping my bubbly wine.

He nods, mimicking me, and I remember something I read in one of those magazines—that if your date copies your body language, they're interested in you. Well, considering I'm leaning forward on my elbows and Samson is doing the same, I'd say he's interested... especially since his eyes keep flitting down to my lips.

"Yeah, this place and a few others, mostly in the city," he answers.

"And your parents are doctors, right?"

"Yes. Pediatricians, actually."

I nod slowly, my lips quirking up. "That makes total sense now. All of you—and what your parents do... it all makes sense."

He leans back and laces his hands behind his head, the white fabric of his shirt taut and clinging to the corded muscles in his arms. "How so?"

I laugh. "Yours have normal jobs, and by proxy, you

seem like the least fucked up of the bunch. Ash is... well... Ash. He has his own issues thanks to the mayor. Ledger is like a walking *fuck you* to his devout parents, and Hunter is the misjudged, angsty son of the headmaster." I sit back, satisfied with my observations.

He smirks. "You think you have us all figured out, but my life has been far from perfect."

I don't have a chance to ask him what he means, because the server brings our food out. Neither of us speaks for a few minutes, inhaling the fresh pasta, the tender steak, and the incredible fish. It's way too much food, but I manage to eat most of it while Samson watches me.

"What's your story, Briar?" he asks, placing his napkin on the table.

I lean back and groan, rubbing my stomach. "I ate too much, if that's what you mean."

He laughs. "No. I mean... before. In California."

I swallow. "Right. California."

He reaches out and takes my hand in his—the soft warmth is comforting, and when his thumb grazes my palm, my skin erupts in goosebumps.

"I know what happened—you don't have to talk about it if you don't want to." I'm about to pull my hand away when he tugs me closer, bringing my hand to his lips again. "I'm sorry for their actions when you first got here. I tried to get them to stop," he explains, his eyes wide and solemn. "And then that day in the quad, when we realized..." He looks down, and when his eyes find mine again, they're swimming with emotion. "He threatened us that day," he laughs. "Said if we messed with you again, that he'd fuck us up," he adds, chuckling.

I ignore the way my throat constricts, how my pulse speeds up at the notion of them all agreeing to at least that. The taunting, the diary, the underwear, the shirt... sure. Those were classic bully moves. But Samson was right—after that day, none of them tried anything questionable.

I lean back and study him, and he watches me with a serious expression.

"Tell me about Micah."

The words must shock him—either he was unaware that I knew, or he wasn't expecting me to ask outright.

"Micah?" he asks, his voice rough. His face is harder now, and the playfulness is gone. "What about him?"

I shrug. "You were dating him when he committed suicide."

Samson grinds his jaw, and his disposition completely changes. "Yeah, and?"

"And there are rumors that you—"

Samson slams his hands on the table, startling me. "Exactly. They're rumors."

I study him, and I notice the flared nostrils, the flushed neck, the furrowed brows.

"You loved him, didn't you?" I ask, leaning forward.

Samson frowns while he picks at a loose thread on his shirt cuff. "Of course I loved him. I'm not a monster."

"Then why does everyone think you bullied him to death?"

This causes him to break, and he sags a bit as he lets out an exasperated breath. "Because, Briar. It's easy to place blame when you know nothing about the situation. When you don't know the people involved. We're human, but we're held up to this standard..." He looks down at his hands and unclenches his fists. "Hunter especially, but us, too, since we're his friends." He pauses, his lips thin. "Micah was sick. And I didn't see the signs until it was too late."

"The sex tape?"

He stares at me. "How do you know about that?"

I shrug. "Scarlett told me."

He looks over my shoulder, his eyes fogging over with nostalgia. "There was a sex tape, yes. I was not the one who released it."

"Who did?"

He shrugs. "We never figured it out, but I suspect it was Micah."

I nod, and we're both quiet for a minute. "Thank you for telling me."

He thumbs his lips, watching me. "It's so much easier to keep people afraid of you—to keep people hating you—than it is to be vulnerable. It's easier to continue the charade. We never corrected people when they made assumptions and look where that got us."

His words are like a dagger to the chest. I reach for his hand, and he lets me take it, giving me a small smile.

"For what it's worth, I don't think you're a monster."

He grins. "Thank you."

He orders us dessert, and then he pays for dinner, like a true gentleman. I can't remember the last time I enjoyed myself on a date. Maybe never. We talk about Paris as we drive to my house, the Sorbonne, and I teach him how to say *fuck you* in French. It's so easy talking to him—and I can be myself completely. When he drops me off, I wait for a second, thinking that maybe he'll kiss me on the doorstep.

But he just grazes my cheek with his lips, gives me a real smile as he walks backward to his car.

"Hey!" I yell, grinning, touching the place on my cheek. "Where's my goodnight kiss?"

He tips his head and smirks as he opens his door. "I never kiss on the first date, Briar."

"But—"

"Trust me," he adds, his eyes darkening. "I won't be so nice next time."

29

BRIAR

I wake up the next morning to the sound of my phone ringing. Rolling over in bed, I glance at the screen and see an unknown number—and the fact that it's barely six in the morning. Groaning, I sit up and press the green button.

"Hello?" I answer, my voice a croak.

"I'm outside."

Ash.

My pulse quickens. "It's early," I whine.

He sniffs, and something uncomfortable slithers down my spine. The asylum—what Samson told me about the Greythorn's...

"I had to get out of the house," he adds.

I jump out of bed, the phone still attached to my ear. "Are you okay?" He doesn't answer, but I know he heard me, because I hear him breathing. "I'll be right down," I add, hanging up and throwing on a pair of leggings. I grab a sweatshirt and my boots, phone, and keys. Once I'm dressed, I quickly brush my teeth and slink down the marble stairs, careful not to wake anyone—though the house is so big that waking someone would probably take a lot more than footsteps on the stairs.

I close the front door behind me and walk to his car—a silver Mercedes G-class. When I climb in and shut the door, I look over at him and my throat constricts.

"Did he do this to you?" I whisper, running my finger over his split lip and black eye.

Ash nods, but he doesn't pull away or flinch at my touch like I expected him to.

"We got in a fight as I was getting ready to go on a run," he explains, and my eyes glide over the jogging pants and long-sleeve athletic shirt that clings to him. "He punched me twice and then stormed out."

I frown. "He's a monster."

Ash shrugs. "I can guarantee I'm not the only child with a monster as a parent."

I shake my head. "I'm sorry."

He wipes his nose and turns to look at me. The light blue of his eyes stands out against the purple of the bruise, and my heart clenches.

"I'm sorry I woke you up," he explains, shifting into drive and pulling out onto the street. "I didn't really want to call any of the guys, you know?"

"I understand. But Hunter should know," I respond, looking out the window.

"I'll tell him later. I didn't—" He pauses, and his fingertips turn white as he grips the steering wheel. "I didn't know who else to call."

He doesn't have to say it. Even the ruthless Kings have feelings. They are human after all, despite being treated like gods. And for someone who is so hated, conflict and turmoil must be isolating with no one to turn to.

"I wish there was something I could do," I say, flicking my eyes to his face.

He looks at me for half a second and smirks. "I can think of something." He puts two fingers in his mouth and licks them vulgarly.

I swat his arm. "Not that."

He shrugs. "I just want to break shit. I'm so sick of playing nice. I want to show him this time, you know? *Really* hurt him."

I run my finger along my lips. "What's his favorite thing?" I ask, pulling a knee into my chest as we head out of town and into the forest.

"His expensive whiskey. His crystal. Anything in his bar—he was a bartender once upon a time, and his status allows him to collect one-of-a-kind pieces..." He stares straight ahead, his eyebrows furrowed.

"I think you just answered your own question," I say, smiling.

He grins and turns us around, skidding on the damp pavement as we pull an illegal U-turn. I screech and grab onto the door handle until we straighten out, and he speeds through the thicket of trees to the outskirts of town.

I'm quiet as he pulls up to his house. It's still early, and fog clings to the mid-century home, so different from the debauchery spilling out of it on Friday night. No lights, no music, no people. It's eerie and beautiful at the same time. He jumps out of the car and comes around to my side, opening the door for me and helping me out. He looks down at my boots and raises an eyebrow.

Pulling me into him, he whispers, "I want to fuck you in those boots one day."

I let out a breathy gasp, but quickly recover. "If you're lucky."

Sonya's words reverberate through my mind.

Find what feels good...

Even a week ago, those words would've stunned me to the point of wanting to leave. But now? They excite me.

I push away from him and walk away as I smile, hearing him come up behind me. He unlocks the door and lets us inside, and there's no pomp and circumstance—no warning—before he takes a large, crystal decanter and smashes it against the wall.

I cover my ears at the sound, but then adrenaline begins to course through me. Grabbing a bottle of liquor, I pour it out on the large shag rug, and then Ash takes the bottle from me, swigging the last little bit before tossing it at the window.

Both the glass—and the window—shatter completely.

I open my mouth in shock, and I can't help the smile on my lips as he hands me another.

And another.

After a minute, I pause, turning to face Ash—who is red-faced and breathing heavily. This is good for him. I know violence can be an unhealthy outlet, and there are probably other ways to channel his rage that aren't so destructive, but I can't help but support him in this.

For him.

For his mom.

"Are you going to get in trouble?" I ask softly, looking

around at the damage. We've destroyed the bar area, and considering we've broken windows, it's going to be a hefty sum to repair.

"I might have," he says slowly, his long fingers curling around the neck of a vodka bottle. "Except I saved the camera footage from our fight earlier on my phone. No one will tolerate seeing the mayor beat the shit out of his son," he adds, watching me with a burning expression.

I give him a wicked smile, and then I pick up another bottle. I can tell by the heaviness and the old, fraying label that this whiskey is old—and probably very expensive. I toss it across the room and yelp as it collides with the television.

Ash chuckles, stepping on glass as he saunters over slowly.

"Good girl." Brushing the tangled hair out of my face, he cocks his head. My breathing halts as he smiles down at me, his lips twisting to the side slightly. "This is so fucking hot."

My breath quickens, my chest rising and falling rapidly, and before I can respond, he pulls me into him and smashes his mouth against mine, hissing briefly and pulling back, touching his cut lip. He must decide it's worth the pain because his lips are back on mine in an instant. My core clenches, and I fist the material of his running shirt, pulling the stretchy fabric until he's flush with my body. It's a flurry of hands, teeth, lips, and nails as I scrape the back of his neck.

He moans, and my body liquifies in his arms. As he moves against me, his hardness pushing against my stomach, my clit pulses with need. I don't wait—reaching up and pulling his shirt off, running my hands over the lean muscles of his abdomen. He may not be as muscular as the others, but he's still fit, still sculpted and easy on the eyes. I groan and pull my sweatshirt off, but he twists me around and presses me against the granite countertop of the bar.

"Briar," he warns, his voice rough and broken.

"Let me make you feel better," I whisper, frantic. I can't tell if I'm being completely selfish or completely *selfless*.

He doesn't wait—just pulls my pants down to my ankles. I step out of my boots and then my pants. I shriek when a palm comes between my legs, spreading me and forcing me apart. I'm panting as he tears into a condom wrapper.

"I have an IUD," I say quickly, backing into him. "Are you clean?"

"Yes," he answers. "You?"

I laugh. "Of course."

"Thank fuck," he whispers. His cock presses against my opening. Using his thick head, he spreads my wetness everywhere, sliding between my slit a couple of times without penetrating me. I arch my back and give him better access, and he presses my abdomen and chest flat against the counter, his hand on the back of my neck so I can't move. I turn my head to the side, my cheek cool against the black granite. "Will you admit it now?" he asks, circling his hips so that his length teases me.

"Admit what?" I breathe, my hands on the edge of the counter, gripping tightly.

"How fucking wet your pussy is for us," he murmurs, his voice so low that I barely hear him.

"I think it's pretty obvious," I chide, and before he can

answer, he slams into me, completely bottoming out inside of me.

I cry out, my body sliding on the hardness of the granite as he pulls out slowly and thrusts into me again.

"Oh fuck," I whimper, my hands coming up to the counter, my fingers splayed on the cool stone to give myself some semblance of control. He tightens his grip around my neck, holding me in place as he continues. My body rocks back and forth with every movement.

"You like it when we tease you," he grits, his breathing heavy. It's a statement, not a question—one I'm beginning to wonder myself. "Your mind may protest, but your body is ours. Admit it."

I keep my mouth closed. I won't surrender to the notion of being *theirs*, but what else could I be? Each of them now has a part of me—two of them have been inside of me. And he's right. I am Play-Doh in their arms.

"Just keep fucking me," I order, grinding my jaw.

He chuckles, loosening his grip on the back of my neck ever so slightly, and I take a deep breath. I wish I could see him—what his face looks like as he pounds into me amidst the broken glass. The look in his eyes, the way his mouth is probably slightly open. I moan, rocking backward so that I can control the tempo. He lets me, and his free hand comes around my stomach. Two fingers begin to work my clit. The smell of it—of my arousal mixed with alcohol—swirls around me. I arch my back into him as he removes his hand from my neck.

"I knew you'd be soaked, but this is a whole new experience," he mutters, the sound of him strumming me getting louder. I fist my hands as my climax draws closer. He's right—I'm so fucking wet. It's dripping down my legs.

The hand that was on my neck slides down to my ass, and his warm, calloused fingers edge closer to my entrance there.

"Ash," I warn, his palm spreading my cheeks.

He spits into his hand, and my body tenses.

"Relax, Briar," he murmurs, his voice low and crooning. "Do you trust me?"

I do. I do trust him. "Yes."

He swirls a finger around and around my ass, and I hold my breath.

"Relax," he commands, circling his hips ever so slightly so that his cock hits the perfect spot inside of me. His other hand continues to strum my clit.

"Oh my god," I cry, closing my eyes. He presses a finger against my ass, not penetrating—just enough pressure to send me over the edge, electrifying parts of me that have never been touched by another human. "Oh my god," I repeat, my pussy grabbing onto his cock as the waves of my orgasm power through me. He inserts a finger into my ass, and I cry out, feeling it against the thin barrier, feeling it everywhere and nowhere at the same time.

Everything intensifies, and my legs shake as another orgasm rips through me, stronger than the last.

"Oh fuck," Ash breathes, inserting another finger into my ass. The feeling of both fingers inside of me is exquisite—to be filled both ways, at the same time, to have his other hand stroking my cunt... "You're making me come, Briar." His voice is undone—raw, ragged, hoarse.

I feel a gush of fluid stream down my legs as I tremble against him, my whole body pulsing with each electric current. Thank God for the counter holding me up. Ash empties into me, stilling as he pulls his hands away and collapses on top of me, his arms forming a cage around me.

"Shit," he whispers, moving the hair off the back of my neck and delicately placing a few kisses along the sensitive spot near the back of my ear.

I can't even speak—I'm still twitching. We push ourselves up, and he quickly bends down and cleans me up. I don't look at him until I've pulled my pants back on. When I do, he's watching me raptly.

"What?" I ask, stepping into my boots.

He walks over to me, erect cock hanging slightly—and *holy fuck*. I scrunch my eyebrows together, confused.

"Did you enjoy it?" There's a bite to his words, and I cock my head.

"Do you really need validation, Ash?" I laugh, crossing my arms. "I thought it was very evident that I did enjoy it."

His eyes sweep down to the puddle where I'd been standing and then they trail back up to my eyes. Something passes over his face—concern or worry of some sort. My eyes fixate on the bruises. And it hits me—he *does* need validation. Today, at least.

I smile and pull him into me. "Yes. That was the best sex I've ever had."

He gives me a cocky grin, reaching around and slapping my ass. "Good. Because I was just warming you up."

My eyebrows shoot up. "How so?"

He tilts his head and walks backward, pulling his pants up quickly.

"You'll see."

30

HUNTER

I'm making myself an Americano when Briar walks into the kitchen. Her wet hair is pulled over one shoulder, and she's wearing a skimpy, silk pajama set that borders on indecent. Averting my eyes and smiling, I hand her a vanilla latte, and she looks down, surprised.

"For me?" she asks, reaching out and taking it.

I nod. "You had an early morning."

She visibly stiffens, her eyes widening just a tiny bit before her stubborn resolve takes over. I literally see the emotions pass over her face—shock that I know, fear that I'm mad, and then regret... as if her fucking my best friend will deter me from pursuing her at all. And then the mask she loves to wear—the ruthless persona she's adopted to protect herself from men like the scum in California who hurt her.

But I see right through it.

Chuckling, I take a couple of steps forward, close enough so that our bodies are touching.

"Do you think I care if you fucked Ash?" I murmur, my lips feathering against her neck. Her eyes flutter closed. "I told you before, fuck one of us, or all of us. They're like my brothers. As long as you're mine when you're with me," I finish, kissing the pale, delicate skin behind her ear.

She looks up at me, her eyes hooded and dark—my hungry, little tempestuous Queen—and smiles. The way her full, pink lips curl up in the corners, the way her face is completely bare of makeup, a light smattering of the palest freckles along the bridge of her nose... I swallow. Why our parents thought we could pretend to be stepsiblings is beyond me.

She's my kryptonite, and I knew the instant we met that staying away from her was never going to be an option.

She's breaking down every barrier I worked hard to build over the last three years, every defense mechanism I've had in place since my mom died. At first, this was all fun and games. Dropping a gorgeous woman into my house, calling her my stepsister, watching as she walked around with such an attitude... It left me intrigued.

Annoyed.

Aroused.

And now that I had a taste of her, now that I know what it feels like to be inside of her, I want more.

I'm just about to kiss her when bare footsteps sound on the wood, and I jump away just as my dad pads into the kitchen.

"Morning, kids," he starts, refilling his mug. He turns to Briar, chuckling. "Your mom is still asleep."

Briar cocks her head and narrows her eyes. "Really? She never sleeps in."

Andrew shrugs. "She was up late organizing our closet. Pretty sure she found clothes in there I haven't worn since the nineties." He turns to face me, and I lean against the counter, crossing my arms. "I thought it would be fun to go apple picking today," he muses, smiling. "As a family."

A small part of me wonders if he knows about Briar and me—if he can sense it. He hasn't been this family friendly since... well, before Mom died.

"Apple picking?" Briar watches Dad with amusement, her eyes twinkling. "How quaint."

I shake my head. Briar obviously loves the idea. I can tell by the way she's impatiently hopping from foot to foot.

"Sure. Fine," I agree.

Briar turns to me. "Apple picking."

I laugh. "That's what he said."

She swats my arm, and my dad mumbles something about waking Aubrey up. When I turn to face Briar, she's watching me behind her large mug of coffee.

"See you in a bit," she says, smirking. "Brother."

31

BRIAR

I dry my hair, run a straightener through it, and then I pull on an oversized sweater and ripped jeans. Tugging my Docs on, I grab my phone and head downstairs, where everyone but my mom is waiting. Andrew is dressed in jeans and a fleece jacket, while Hunter is wearing faded jeans, boots, and a white T-shirt. He has his black leather jacket in his hands—the same one he wore that first day at school, with the ribbed material on the arms. I'm just about to ask where my mom is when she comes up behind me, smiling at everyone.

"This is so exciting," she beams, throwing an arm around my shoulders. "Our first family outing." She's wearing an outfit like mine; except she has on skinny jeans and sneakers with her sweater. She looks over at me and grins. "You look nice, sweetheart." Something about the way she says it, and the way her eyes flit between Hunter and me, like she's in on our secret...

I plaster on a fake smile for her, and then I look at Hunter, who is trying so hard not to laugh.

He thinks this is hilarious, doesn't he? Brother and sister out for a day of apple picking and family fun... except the brother and the sister fucked like rabbits on Friday night.

Except he isn't my brother, is he? We didn't even know each other before ten days ago, so I feel like we deserve some credit for that.

"We can't forget to take a picture for our Christmas card," my mom croons, unlocking the Subaru as we all climb in.

Yeah, this isn't going to be awkward *at all*.

I climb into the back seat as Hunter drops into the other side, that cocky smile still pasted on his lips. I glare at him again, and he just shakes with laughter. I'm so glad my discomfort brings him amusement.

"What should we listen to?" my mom asks, her hand resting gently on Andrew's as he navigates us out of the driveway.

Hunter and I both mumble something unintelligible, and just as I click into the seatbelt, Hunter's hand slips onto my thigh.

I widen my eyes. How dare he? I flick my eyes to the front seat quickly, shoving his hand off of me. He just chuckles, and I spend the next thirty minutes uncomfortable and acutely aware of the guy next to me, who's face as we came together is burned into my memory.

"Briar?" my mom asks from up front. "Can you hear us?"

I snap out of my daydream and clear my throat. "Sorry, what?"

"One of Hunter's short stories was accepted by the *New Yorker*," Andrew answers proudly.

I look at Hunter, who is gazing out the window. "What? It was? When?"

"This morning," he answers, turning to face me.

"You didn't say anything earlier," I add, flushed. "Congratulations!"

"Thanks." He shrugs and tilts his head, smiling. "Sis," he adds.

"It's very commendable," my mom continues, looking back at us. "Have you thought about moving to New York for college? Maybe one of those small, liberal arts schools would really nurture your writing."

He shrugs again, and I have to laugh. He's so broody, like he enjoys being melancholy even though his life is very, very comfortable. Even so, The *New Yorker* is a huge deal. I don't know anything about writing, and even I know of the *New Yorker*.

"I've thought about it. I kind of want to take a year off and write a book," he explains, clearing his throat.

"We have time to talk about it," Andrew interjects, and the two of them begin chatting as we pull onto a dirt driveway leading into a cute-as-hell orchard.

After we park, I get out and look around as Mom, Andrew, and Hunter begin walking to the ticket counter. Andrew pays, purchasing the large buckets for picking, and then he tells us to team up. Taking my mom's hand, they walk away excitedly, leaving Hunter and me alone at the entrance.

Hundreds of large apple trees are lined up in perfect

rows. The sun is strong, but it's not hot at all. In fact, the air has that potent *autumn* smell to it today—a little bit of burning wood, cinnamon, and crisp air. Add in the scent of sweet apples, and this is a *fall-gasm* if I ever saw one. Our falls were mild in California, but every few years, we were blessed with a decent autumn.

"So, the *New Yorker*," I say as we walk deeper into the orchard. There aren't very many people here, and the people we see are all preoccupied with filling up their buckets.

Hunter groans. "It's not that big of a deal. It's just a small piece I wrote over the summer."

"Can I read it sometime?" I ask, shielding my face from the sun.

Hunter stops walking, turning to face me with a frown. "You really want to?"

I laugh. "Of course. Why would I ask if I didn't really want to read it?"

I'm about to apologize for being so pushy when he reaches down and pries the bucket from my hand, setting it down. He gently pushes me up against one of the trees, hiding us from view. I open my mouth in surprise, but he bends down and his lips crash against mine, his breath sweet, his lips velvety soft. He pulls away a few inches, breathing heavily.

"It's like you're a zipper," he says slowly, running a finger down the middle of my chest, mimicking the movement. "You go your whole life zipped up, and then someone comes along and starts to tug. Inevitably, you'll be unzipped—and you won't be prepared for what spills out. That's how I feel when I'm around you."

I quirk my lips up slightly. "Yeah, I can definitely tell you're a writer."

He laughs and kisses me again, our bodies rocking against each other, our tongues sliding, our hands fisting. I moan when he bends down and grabs my ass cheeks, pulling my core into his hard length poking through his jeans.

"We shouldn't... Not here."

"What, you don't want Mom and Dad to see us kissing?" he jokes, and I shove him away.

Walking back to my bucket, I pick it up and continue down the lane of trees. We're quiet as we pick, with Hunter helping me grab the higher fruit I can't quite reach. After we've filled our buckets, we set them down and sit under the shade of one of the larger trees, each eating a sweet yet slightly sour apple. I must say, fresh apples are *so* much better than store bought—the tangy acidity compliments the sweetness, and it's so crisp that the flesh cleaves away cleanly with each bite.

"So how will this work?" I ask, curiosity eating at me.

He must understand what I'm asking—how I'm going to come to terms with the fact that I'm essentially dating all of them at once—because he smiles and shrugs.

"We each get our share of you," he muses. "We protect you. Show you that sex can feel good again. Date you, fuck you, worship you..."

My body heats. I can't justify cutting any of them loose—can't fathom *not* seeing where it goes with each of them. And none of them seem to be jealous. Sonya's words really resonated with me. I need to listen to my intuition. I need to follow my heart, and right now, my heart cannot possibly choose.

He chuckles, the sound low and throaty. "Do I get jealous? Maybe a little. But not enough for me to ask you to stop," he answers, looking at me with furrowed brows. "I don't expect you to be beholden to me and only me, Briar."

"Yeah, but—"

"Listen," he says, his eyes dark as he leans in closer. I get a whiff of vetiver, the wind carrying it over to me. "You're allowed to date or fuck whoever you want. Well, that's not true—I prefer it was one of the guys, since I can vouch for every single one of them, and I know they'll take care of you."

So, the devil has a heart after all.

"And if I hadn't told you about my past?" I ask, my voice quiet.

He looks down at his hands. "I don't know, honestly. I think we were scared. No one—and I mean no one—had ever challenged us like you did. I can't say for sure, but I do know that all of us felt something the first time we saw you. And I think we assumed you'd label us monsters, so why bother acting nice, you know?"

"I was angry when my father told me you and your mom were moving in. That first day in the park, when we called you our little lamb? We were drinking, being idiots, and I wanted to push you away. I wanted you to leave. Except, I didn't expect what you did. Most women would've run away or called the cops after seeing four guys in hoods in the dark... but not you. You stayed, and then you kept walking, like it was nothing. It was like watching a car wreck. You don't necessarily *want* to look, but you do it anyways, because you want to see what happens when you do. That's what it was like for us those first few days."

I shrug. "Well, none of you ever scared me. You all

wore your attitudes on your shoulder, so I knew what I was getting myself into from the get-go. I'm way more terrified of men who hide their monstrosities."

Hunter's eyes slide to mine, and he reaches for my hand. "I'm here if you ever want to talk about it. But I also don't expect a recounting of what happened. It's your story to tell."

I swallow thickly, trying not to cry. My hands are shaking as I place them on my thighs, turning to face Hunter again.

"My—my mom's ex raped me," I whisper, my voice uneven. "And then I stabbed him with a kitchen knife."

Hunter's mouth twitches, and he nods. "I truly hope you killed him," he muses.

No one besides my mom ever made me feel like I did the right thing, but Hunter... I am grateful for him.

My lips tilt up into a smile. "Not quite. They revived him, and he's in jail."

I think back to that night, as painful as it is. He raped me, and while he was inside of me, while his hand was over my mouth, I'd reached around and grabbed the kitchen knife I'd been using to chop vegetables. I'd stabbed him in the neck, and he'd fallen onto the floor. I can still see the puddle of blood soaking through his light blue shirt.

And then I ran.

A few hours later, the doctor interrogated me. They did a rape kit, and confirmed it was Cam.

But the police—his friends? They never believed me. They said it was consensual. And then the rumors started, saying I'd lied.

Saying *I'd* done something wrong by tempting him.

My mom had gotten us out of there as quickly as possible. There was a trial, and he was sentenced to thirteen years since I was a minor at the time.

It didn't stop the rumors, though.

I kept my head down, my mom lost customers, and then we left everything behind.

She met Andrew at the perfect time.

"He was so nice to me," I continue, pulling my knees up into my chest. "He'd been dating my mom for a few months. I'd never gotten a bad vibe from him. He was funny, kind, and he cooked us dinner every weekend." Hunter is watching me with careful concern. His eyes are harder now—darker, somehow. "We were hanging out in our apartment. My mom was gone—coordinating a wedding in Utah—and he texted me about coming over. I didn't think anything of it. I never met my father, and I liked the idea of hanging out with Cam... like a father/daughter thing, you know?" My voice breaks, and I look away.

I shake my head. When I look back at Hunter, his jaw is clenched, but he doesn't say anything. He just listens.

"He'd been acting sort of weird—touchy-feely, and he offered me wine, but again, I thought that maybe this was normal. I had no precedent, nothing to compare what a normal relationship like that was like. I thought maybe he was attempting to be cool."

"It's not normal," Hunter growls. "He is a predator."

"I was in the kitchen chopping zucchini when he came up behind me. I was wearing a dress—something I now regret. Pants would've been a better barrier—"

"Don't you dare blame your *outfit*, Briar," Hunter fumes, his nostrils flaring.

I tilt my head and rest my cheek on my knee. "I was

surprised. He'd never shown that kind of interest in me. And I thought perhaps it was a misunderstanding. So, I asked him to stop. But he held me against the counter and things got out of control."

"You asked him to stop, and he didn't. That's rape," Hunter growls. "He's lucky he's behind bars." His jaw is taut, and he releases his fisted hands a few times, splaying them over his pants like he doesn't trust himself not to punch something.

I smile, lifting my head and pulling his hand to my chest.

"Anyway, he... raped me. I tried fighting, but he was strong. As he... finished... I reached over and grabbed the knife. He almost slapped it out of my hand, but he was distracted—his phone was ringing—so I was able to twist around and stab him."

"I thought I killed him. It wasn't until later that night, after my stint in the hospital, that I found out. They couldn't get him to wake up. He'd lost forty percent of his blood, and his body was in shock. But after a couple of hours of being in a coma, he woke up. The trial was a couple of months later, and because of the evidence, he was sentenced to thirteen years."

Hunter shakes his head. "He deserves to be dead."

I nod. "I know."

He stands, pulling me up the next second. I brush myself off and reach down for my apple bucket. When I straighten, he's watching me with a dark, concerned expression.

I sigh. "I promise, I'm okay."

"I was a little rough with you—"

"Stop," I murmur. "I liked it, Hunter. Cam didn't ruin

sex for me. I'm strong as fuck. My mom sent me to the best psychologist in the bay area. I feel... okay. Sonya taught me how to claim my sexuality, how to take my pleasure back. Through healing, I've learned what I like and what I don't like. And I can assure you, I like you—all of you."

He smiles, grabbing my bucket and placing it on top of his.

"Good. Because now that I've tasted you..." he gives me a long, heated look before walking away, carrying both buckets. His muscles strain against the leather, but it doesn't faze him that he's carrying at least forty pounds of apples.

I cock my head and watch him walk away, admiring the way his jeans sculpt the back of his thighs. Sighing, I follow.

32

BRIAR

After spending nearly two hours getting caught up on homework—Ravenwood Academy's college prep curriculum is no joke—I spend the rest of the evening with my mom. Andrew is working, and Hunter is out with Ledger, but I feel like vegging out in front of the TV. We watch Friends down in the basement, since Hunter and I resolved our territorial issues, and I tell her about the other guys. I don't go into detail, obviously, but I think she suspects something's going on with Hunter. We talk about my classes, and she tells me about the new couch she ordered for the living room. It's nice to just hang out with her away from Andrew and Hunter.

Around ten, she heads up to bed, kissing me on the top of the head before retreating. I continue watching season seven alone with some of Hunter's chocolate.

I shoot Ash a quick text asking how he is, and he responds almost immediately.

I'm staying at Samson's. Haven't heard from my father, so either he's still not home, or he got the hint with the video surveillance footage I sent him from our fight.

I hit the call button, and he answers straight away. "Hey," he says, his voice gravelly. I hear Samson murmur something in the background. "What are you doing right now?"

I pause, looking down at myself. I'm clad in my new pajamas from earlier—a silk camisole and shorts.

"Nothing, just watching TV. I wanted to check on you."

He's quiet for a beat, and I can tell my question catches him off guard. "I'm fine," he answers quickly. "You should come over," he adds, his voice low.

I sigh. "It's a school night."

I hear him hand the phone to Samson. "Come on, Briar," Samson begs. "We have brownies. Fresh baked."

Dammit. These guys have only known me for a week, and it seems they've already discovered my weakness.

"Fine."

I hang up, and Samson texts me his address. I hop up and turn the TV off, heading upstairs and changing into jogger pants and a sweatshirt. I pull a pair of sneakers on before shooting a quick text to my mom that I'm heading to Samson's with the guys for a bit. I know it's late, but I don't have a curfew. When I turned eighteen over the summer, we agreed that if I was transparent about where I was and who I was with, I could go anywhere, anytime.

I'm sure if Samson and Ash weren't Hunter's best

friends, she might have more of a problem with it. But I think she trusts Hunter—trusts that he and his friends will keep me safe. After all, her own brother took care of her when she got pregnant

She texts me back.

Be safe. I love you.

I set my phone down and look in the mirror, tilting my head as I study myself. *What am I doing?* It's a school night. I think I know these guys, but do I *really* know them? Sitting on the edge of my bed, I shoot Sonya a quick text, even though it's late, asking her how I'll know if its intuition driving me, or something silly, like lust. Relief washes through me when she responds.

You'll know it's intuition when you feel relief at having made that choice. For example, you say you're not sure if you should go to Samson's house. Why? Do you trust them? Have they ever given you a reason not to trust them? Think about calling back and saying no. Would you be relieved? Or disappointed? I don't want you to feel like you're being forced to hang out with two guys from school, but there will come a day when you'll have to relinquish control a little. Sometimes the best memories are made with sporadic decisions. Follow your gut, Briar. I won't be around forever, so you're going to need to fine tune your instincts, you know? Evaluate your surroundings. Listen to your gut. Apply common sense.

I smile as I head downstairs and get into my car. She's right. The second Ash asked me to come over, I was *excited*. I've never feared them—not even that first day in the park.

I drive the two miles to Samson's house, which I'd been to briefly after Hunter and I dropped him off the night of Ash's party. His house sits at a slightly higher elevation in the hills surrounding the main part of town. Ornate, large, ostentatious. Parking in the circular driveway, I walk up to the door, and it opens just as I walk up the steps.

Ash smiles at me and lets me through, closing the door behind me. My eyes flit across the house. Do all rich people have the same decorators? My mom would have a field day remodeling this basic, beige mess. I look at Ash, wincing when I realize his bruises are so much worse than they were this morning. His cut lip is more pronounced, too. He's in sweats and a T-shirt.

"Ash," I chide, reaching up to his face. "You should be icing that."

He takes my hand and kisses it. "I'm fine. I promise."

"There she is," Samson says, sauntering up to us. He's wearing plaid pajama pants, and it startles me to see both of them so casual. "Who's up for the hot tub?" he smirks, crossing his arms. The biceps are pushed up with his hands, and I swallow.

"I didn't bring a suit," I huff. They look at each other and smile. "Hell no," I whine, frowning.

"We promise to behave," Samson says, gesturing for me to follow him.

"I can make no such promises," Ash muses, and we all walk through the living area, back to the kitchen, and then out to the back yard. "Besides, I've been inside of you," he murmurs, his voice low enough so that only I hear.

"So that's why you invited me over?" I ask them both, crossing my arms.

"No. I invited you over to show you this," Samson

answers, and I gasp when he moves out of the way, showing me the view.

An infinity pool decked out in rainbow lights sits before us. And above it, a jacuzzi cut into the stone, with a waterfall cascading into it. The cityscape before us is incredible—we can see all of Greythorn, including some of the forest and the other parts of Massachusetts beyond it. I take a step forward, my mouth hanging open.

"Holy shit," I whisper, looking at Samson. "I love it." I turn to Ash. "You're both assholes who knew I couldn't say no." I pin him with a serious expression. "And I expect brownies as a reward later."

Samson snorts. "You got it." He gestures to the pool. "Come on. Let's go. You only live once, right?"

Fucking right.

"Where are your parents?" I ask, looking at the house behind me.

"They're not here," Samson answers cryptically, smirking.

Sometimes the best memories are made with sporadic decisions.

I sigh and walk over to one of the chairs, disposing of my purse and stepping out of my shoes. Samson and Ash follow me, and soon we're all naked.

I'm too distracted by the pool to pay attention—and I've already seen Ash naked from the waist down—but Samson surprises me.

He has a cock piercing, and the guy is *hung*.

He must see me admiring his package, and he gives me a shy smile before running and jumping into the pool. I put my hands on my hips, waiting for Ash to do the same.

"You first," he says, his voice low, eyeing my peaked,

hard nipples. It's not exactly warm tonight, which doesn't help the situation.

I flip him off before jumping in, the cold water shocking me at first. When I surface, Samson is placing his glasses on the side of the pool. Without them, he looks less innocent—and more like the other guys. Darker, edgier—like a whole new person. He swims over to me as I wipe my face with my hand.

"Are you having fun yet?" he asks, his voice low.

Ash jumps into the pool, but I don't look up. Samson is watching me like a vulture—a look I've never seen on his face before.

"You promised to be good," I murmur, treading water and giggling.

"I know. And I'll keep that promise as long as you want me to."

Forever the gentleman.

"This water is fucking cold," Ash barks, swimming over.

"You'll get used to it," Samson jokes, splashing him.

"Dude, fuck off," Ash growls, wiping his face. "Let's go in the jacuzzi."

I watch as he exits the pool, admiring the sculpted muscles of his ass. His legs are long and lean, and the muscles in his back contract with every step. I look at Samson, and it appears I'm not the only one admiring Ash's backside.

"How can you see without your glasses?" I ask, splashing him playfully.

He chuckles. "I'm far-sighted. I can see things far away, just not up close."

I smirk. "But you *were* admiring his ass," I tease.

He cocks his head. "And? I'm not ashamed that I find him attractive, and he knows it."

Heat flares through me. "You and Ash?" I ask, glancing up at the jacuzzi. Ash is sitting in the water with his head back and eyes closed.

Samson smiles—his teeth are so white, so straight. He's beautiful—the way the water drips off his pale skin, the way his coppery eyes look gold from the pool lights.

"You guys have…"

Samson nods. "A few times. He's not quite out of the closet though. Whereas I'm proudly bi."

I pull my lip between my teeth, imagining the two of them. I squeeze my legs together—something that's not so easy to do while trying to stay afloat.

"Love is love," I concede, grinning.

"It's definitely not love with Ash. Just fun. Though I do love him as a friend."

"And what about me?" I ask, swimming a little farther away.

Samson's lips twitch slightly. "What about you, Briar?"

"Could you see yourself loving me? Or am I just a fun time?"

His eyes darken slightly, his face turning serious. My breathing hitches at that look, and I can't take my eyes off him.

"You're both. Neither. I don't know how to explain it. I feel like…" He shakes his head.

"What?" I ask, changing my mind and swimming closer. He inhales sharply when my hand brushes his abdomen.

"I feel like an animal around you," he says, his voice gravelly. "I am a feminist, I believe in women's rights, and consent, and all of that..." He swallows, and I admire the way his throat bobs. "But you make me wild. *Feral*," he growls.

I smile, reaching down and gripping his firm length.

He hisses, surprised. And he's rock hard.

"Are you guys coming in or what?" Ash yells from across the pool.

"Yeah," I answer, letting go of Samson and swimming to the stairs.

Walking out, I saunter to the jacuzzi, sitting across from Ash. He gives me a closed-mouthed, lecherous smile. I'm about to make a snide remark when Samson climbs in.

Holy...

Ash must notice Samson's hard on too because his eyes flit from me to him, and something akin to lust passes over his face. Samson sits next to Ash, and even though I'm in a jacuzzi, my entire body tingles as they stare at each other.

"Is that for me or for her?" Ash asks, swallowing.

Samson smiles and looks between us. "Both, I think."

A tremor of excitement runs through me when Ash reaches out and brushes a piece of wet hair off Samson's forehead. And then he pins his eyes on me.

"Get over here," he commands.

Fuck.

33

Briar

I slowly drift over, bracing myself. I sit next to Ash, and he quickly pulls me into his lap. His hard length presses into my ass cheek.

"Didn't I tell you earlier that I was warming you up?"

My heart pounds against my ribs. "Yes," I breathe.

"Well, this is the real deal. You ready?"

I nod a little too vigorously. Just as I'm about to ask how something like this starts, Samson brushes my nipple as he moves to a spot in front of me.

"Which one of us do you want where, Briar?" Ash asks.

I look between them. How can I possibly choose something like that? Who has to make that kind of decision in real life?

Is this real life?

Before I can answer, Samson takes my hands and presses himself against me, placing his lips on mine.

They're buttery soft, and his tongue nudges my lips apart, asking for access. I groan when he bites my lower lip, and his hands come to my face as he continues to kiss me. I stand, and Ash follows suit, coming up behind me and rocking his cock up into me, moving my hair off my neck and kissing me there. His body is firm behind me, and Samson pushes himself against the front of me, his hard abdomen against mine.

Holy shit.

"Briar," Ash purrs. "Where do you want me?"

I pull away from Samson, tipping my head back as Ash kisses my neck from behind.

"I want to see you two together first."

Samson slowly moves away from me, backing up against the other wall of the jacuzzi. He's smiling at Ash.

"Well? Let's show her how we do this. Unless you're scared."

Fire ravages my body as Ash swims over, gripping the back of Samson's hair and pulling it backward.

"You don't fucking scare me, Hall," Ash growls. And then he smashes his lips against Samson's, and I have to squeeze my legs together as I watch them writhe against each other—hard muscle, smooth skin, wet hair. Ash pulls away, breathing heavily. "Stand on the step."

Glad I'm not the only one he loves to boss around.

Samson's eyes are darker now, his face serious. He stands up, his erection taught, causing the cock piercing to stick out slightly. I lean back in my seat and spread my legs, my fingers drifting downwards to the slick wetness between them. I begin to circle my clit with two fingers as Ash grips Samson's ass and places his mouth around Samson's cock.

Samson groans, throwing his head back and grabbing Ash's hair as Ash slides his lips down to the base of his cock.

Shit.

My hands move faster as Ash ups his tempo, his hand coming underneath Samson's balls, stroking him there.

Samson cries out, putting his hands behind his head. And then he looks at me.

"You like this?" he bites out, thrusting slightly into Ash's mouth. "Seeing Ash on his knees with my dick in his mouth?"

I nod, biting my lower lip as I arch my back and close my eyes.

"Stop."

My eyes fly open, and Ash is next to me now. Samson is stroking his cock, watching us. "Do you really think we're going to let you come by yourself? Or without you?"

I open my mouth to respond, but he stands up and gestures for me to follow him out of the jacuzzi. I look at Samson, who just nods.

We all walk over to the large lounge set, decked out with an outdoor daybed made of thick, white linen. Ash stops and points to it, so I climb onto my back and wait.

"I'll be right back."

He walks away, and I turn to find Samson standing next to me.

"That was the single hottest thing I've ever seen," I laugh, suddenly feeling very exposed. Samson must notice because he climbs into the bed and hovers above me.

"Just wait," he whispers, bending down and kissing my neck. I tilt my head backward and give him access, moving underneath him and closing my eyes. I can feel his firmness, feel it touching the side of my hip, so I buck them upwards and spread my legs, waiting.

"Please," I whisper.

His warm hand slides down, gripping the flesh on my side. His lips graze mine, and I gasp when his hand spreads me farther.

"What did Ash mean earlier?" he mumbles, planting kisses along my jawline. "About warming you up?"

"I'm back," Ash says, a few feet away. He places a bottle of lubricant on the table.

"Ah," Samson purrs, knocking my legs apart with his knee. "I should've known." He's breathing heavily, and out of the corner of my eye, I see Ash douse his cock in lube, the sound exhilarating. "Watch us," Samson whispers, pushing the thick head of his length against me. "Watch as I fuck you." The cool metal against my skin is electrifying, and I moan, low and deep. And then he enters me, sliding in smoothly, filling me completely.

I gasp, and he hisses—I try to accommodate his girth, but there's no point. It burns, but the burning soon gives way to immense fullness.

"Holy shit," Samson whispers, his voice husky and uneven. "You're so fucking tight."

And then pulls out, and I can feel every inch of him thanks to his piercing. It slides against the spot inside of me, the sensations new and incredible. Driving back into me, I cry out. He does this a few more times—until I begin to meet him with every thrust. And then he rolls and flips me in one swift movement, so that I'm on top of him. I place my knees on either side of him, riding his cock slowly as he throws his head back.

Ash comes up behind me, placing a warm hand on my

ass. I look back, and a nervous tremor works its way down my spine.

"If you need to stop, tell us to stop," Ash murmurs, his voice thick. He spreads my cheeks with his hand. "Just like before, remember?"

I nod, looking down at Samson. He's moving underneath me, thrusting into me from below. Ash hands him something silver, and I don't register what it is until he turns it on. He gently presses the world's tiniest vibrator against my clit, and my whole body convulses on top of him.

"This will make it easier," he murmurs, rubbing it in slow circles. "Breathe, Briar."

I'm about to ask him what he means when I feel Ash's cock against my other opening, and I immediately clench up.

"Breathe," Samson repeats. When I look back down at him, I take a few steadying breaths. His bottom lip is between his teeth, and *God,* he is so beautiful. I smile and close my eyes, breathing heavily as Ash's cock presses into me again. This time, I don't protest. Because of the lube, it slides in easily, and I let out a loud breath of air as I feel him inside of me, stretching me. It stings a little, and I'm grateful that he isn't moving yet.

"Holy shit, I can fucking feel you," Samson grinds out, looking at Ash over my shoulder.

Those words reverberate through me, and I nudge Samson's hand with the vibrator. He chuckles as he moves it quicker, and then I hear a click right before it gets stronger.

"Oh fuck, yes," I moan, propping myself up on my elbows over Samson as he moves slowly inside of me. Ash grunts, and I rock my hips just slightly. Ash begins to move, and Samson ups the vibration one more time.

I think I'll probably shoot straight up into the sky when I come.

"You good?" Ash asks, a hand on my ass again. He moves into me slowly, but it doesn't hurt anymore. Now... now it just feels so full, *so* good...

"Yeah," I whisper. "God, yeah."

Samson swirls the vibrator against my clit, moving it to where we're joined and back up to my hood again, sliding between my swollen vulva.

"Oh my god," I cry, my hands turning into fists.

"This is incredible," Ash murmurs. "I can feel both of you at the same time."

"You're going to make me come," Samson growls, speeding up and working into me harder now.

Ash does the same—so that they're both slamming into me at the same time. The friction from the vibrator builds my climax so high, it's almost painful. I can't speak, can't move, as Samson rubs me with the silver bullet. I've never felt this much—the piercing, both cocks inside of me, the vibrator—and my legs begin to quake violently. The intensity builds, and I cry out loudly now, clawing at the fabric, at Samson's arms, trying to hold on to something before I go flying off the rails.

"I'm going to come," Samson says, his voice throaty. "Oh fuck, I'm going to come," he says again, baring his teeth.

"Me too," Ash growls, placing another hand on my other ass cheek and plowing into me with zero abandon now. I look back at him, his face blazing. They both groan, the sound causing me to convulse with pleasure, and then—

"Me three," I cry, the climax spilling over and running through each muscle, contracting and pulsing, my one giant muscle releasing all tension in a long, intense seism. I feel a gush of liquid rush between my legs, my body still gripping their rock-hard cocks firmly as the pulsing stops. I look down to see Samson watching me raptly, his chest wet.

"Holy fuck," he whispers, sweating and panting. "You came all over me, little lamb."

"Breathe," Ash commands, pulling out of me slowly.

Now *that* is the weirdest feeling ever.

Samson helps me sit up, pulling out and cleaning me with a washcloth Ash must've grabbed when he got the lube and vibrator.

"That was…"

Ash comes to lie next to me, so that I'm in the middle.

"Incredible," Samson answers.

"Fucking hot," Ash adds, and we all laugh. "Are you okay?"

I pause before answering. Not because I'm unsure, but because I've never been surer about anything in my life.

Whatever happened that first day in Ravenwood Academy tethered them to me—all four of them, all at once. And oddly, it's comforting to know that I have four guys who seem to want to take care of me, to give me pleasure, to ensure I am safe and comfortable and happy.

For the first time, I have no doubts that I am okay.

As long as I am with them.

"Yeah," I answer. "I'm more than okay."

34

Briar

The next day at school, I brace myself for the onslaught of questions from Scarlett and Jack. I don't want to be dishonest with them, but I also know the situation I'm in is... unconventional. Then again, they're both open-minded, so it's possible that they won't even care, especially if I explain the change in attitude with regards to the Kings. I pull up to the parking lot and find a space in the back row, and just as I put the car in park, I hear tapping on the glass of the passenger side.

I roll my window down and stare at Ledger.

"Hi?"

He leans on my door, the sleeves of his button-up rolled up to his elbows, showing off his tan, corded forearms that are scattered with various tattoos.

"This isn't your spot anymore," he says, looking at me like I just committed a faux pas.

"What do you mean?" I ask, looking around. "We don't have assigned spots."

He gives me a lopsided smile. "You do now. Follow me."

I start my engine and pull out, and when I loop around the parking lot, he directs me to a spot between the four cars.

Sighing, I pull in between Ash and Hunter's car,

I turn the engine off and climb out, grabbing my backpack. When I pivot to face the school after locking up, I'm met with stares from everyone still mingling in the lot.

Great.

"Come on," Ledger says, guiding me to the gate with a gentle hand on my back.

"I don't need to be chaperoned through campus," I joke, rolling my eyes.

Turning to face me, he smirks down at me. "Is that what you think I'm doing?" His blonde hair is hanging down one side of his face, and his navy pants cling to the thick muscles in his legs. He doesn't look eighteen. He looks twenty-five—especially with the ink. I ignore the way everyone has quieted, watching us as we interact, but I don't think any of them will be able to hear what we're saying.

"I don't know. I just don't want to be treated differently."

He shrugs. "You're one of us now. It would be strange if you didn't park with us. I figured you'd enjoy being near the front gate."

That is true.

I shift my weight from one hip to the other. "Fine."

He smirks, rubbing his bottom lip with his thumb as

his blue eyes find mine. "You're not beholden to us just because you park with us. Go be with your friends," he says, smiling. And then he turns and walks away, and I'm left to ignore the lingering gazes as I make my way to the quad.

Scarlett is sitting with Jack when I walk up, and as I do, Jack lets out a whistle.

"Someone was busy this weekend," he jokes.

I shrug. "I have to tell you something," I start, looking between them. Just as I open my mouth, the bell rings. "At lunch, okay?"

"Fine," Jack whines, standing. "But I want all the deets."

◈

The fifty minutes spent in pre-calculus go by so slowly, and I don't notice the way every seat surrounding me is empty until I get up to leave as the bell rings. Swallowing, I look around at my classmates, and sure enough, none of them meets my eye. I quickly gather my things and leave, shaking my head.

In French class, it's the same thing. No one wants to sit next to me, and no one makes eye contact. It's like I'm invisible. I'm walking through the hallways toward lunch when people start whispering, parting the walkway down the middle for me to pass.

Is this what it's like for the guys? Do they just play into the stereotype everyone has them in? Because even as my eyes land on another student, they must mistake my confusion for intimidation. They look down—and they look...

Just like they do when Hunter and the guys walk by.

The Kings aren't bullies. Not really. But people presume they are, and that's where their reputation comes into play.

It's so much easier to keep people afraid of you—to keep people hating you—than it is to be vulnerable. It's easier to continue the charade. We never corrected people when they made assumptions and look where that got us.

"I'm not contagious," I mutter, rolling my eyes.

A girl with thick, black curls and a pretty face shakes her head as she leans against the lockers. "You're their property now."

I whirl to face her. "I'm no one's property," I reply, cocking my head. "They don't own me."

She matches my stance, pushing off the locker and standing in front of me. "That's what you think."

Her words rattle me, but I continue out of the building toward the quad. When I spot Jack sitting with Scarlett, I perk up, skipping over to them. But as I approach, Jack looks over his shoulder and glares at me.

"What?" I ask innocently.

Scarlett crosses her arms. "We know what you did."

My heart leaps into my throat. "How?"

Jack laughs. "She's not even trying to deny it." Then he turns to me. "It's your funeral, not mine, so you do you, boo."

"What are you talking about?" I beg, sitting next to them.

Scarlett looks at me, her expression pained. "I don't think you should sit here with us today."

My body turns to ice, and my eyes flit between them.

"I don't really understand why you're mad at me. Out of everyone, I thought you'd both understand."

Is it the fact that I slept with them? Or is it something else?

"You're new, Briar," Jack grits out. "You have no idea what they're capable of. You've only been here a week. I've known them my whole life."

My eyes sting with tears. "I'm really confused. Are we talking about how I slept with them?"

"*Them?*" Jack asks, eyeing me suspiciously.

"It doesn't matter who you fuck. Personally, I don't care as long as it's consensual," Scarlett hisses, looking around at the people staring at us. "But Greythorn is a small town. Micah was our best friend. We can never forgive Samson for what he did to Micah, but apparently that doesn't matter to you. I think you're making a mistake. I mean, there are rumors that you vandalized Medford Asylum. You've got balls, considering Christopher Greythorn is certifiably insane. Oh, and by the way, we didn't want to go to that stupid party on Friday. But we did—for you."

It's like cold water spills over my body, and I stare at Scarlett. "How did you know about Medford—"

"Have you checked your phone, Briar?" Jack asks, his voice quiet.

I quickly pull my phone out. It's been on silent since I left the house, but he's right. I have texts from my mom, from Andrew, from Hunter...

"I don't understand," I mumble, feeling my vision tilt a bit.

"The police arrested Ash a few minutes ago. Took him straight from class. I guess his father figured out what happened."

Fury burns through me, hot and potent. "Do the police also know that Christopher Greythorn beats his son?"

Also, why wasn't anyone else caught? We were all there...

"He's the mayor, Briar—he has the potential to ruin my family's business, and we need all the business we can get," she adds, referring to Romancing the Bean. A small pang of guilt runs through me. I didn't even think about that. "Look, I really don't care if you want to sow your wild oats with all of them. But Samson Hall is dangerous." She pauses. "If I'm caught associating with Greythorn's newest criminal... I guess I just thought you were smarter than that."

Jack nods, and his eyes flit to something over my shoulder. "Your keepers are here. See you later, Briar." He and Scarlett get up and walk away, and I hate the way his voice sounds so disappointed—how they both sound disappointed.

Maybe I should've been smarter. Maybe I should've said no to vandalizing Medford, to smashing Christopher's nice things at the house.

I twist around as Hunter, Ledger, and Samson stroll toward me, their expressions hard.

"They arrested Ash?" I ask, crossing my arms.

"Let's go," Hunter growls. He doesn't answer my question—just grabs my hand and pulls me toward the gate. Everyone is staring—all their eyes are on us. When I look at Samson, his lips are a tight line. Ledger, too—they're all expressionless, but I can see the minute details that tell me they're beyond pissed off.

The security guard doesn't even balk as we approach the gate. He just lets us through.

The Kings, always getting what they want.

I glance at Hunter, and he looks down at me, blazing fury written all over his face. I pull away from him and stop a few feet from our cars.

"What happened?" I ask, glancing between their three faces. "I thought we made sure there were no security cameras at Medford?"

Hunter's lips quirk just slightly, but then the anger reappears, causing his brows to furrow together.

"Ash will be fine," he says, and the other guys let out exasperated sighs. "Christopher is in deep shit, considering Ash sent the police department footage of their fight. He got his dad in full view, beating the shit out of him. No matter what happens with Medford, the fact that the mayor is on video abusing his child will never be forgiven. Mission accomplished," he murmurs. "Ash was the only one identified. I guess we missed a camera somewhere. They might not have identified us yet, but everyone knows we were there too."

Dread fills me, and I swallow thickly. "It's only a matter of time before they do," I murmur, crossing my arms.

Will this jeopardize my future? The Sorbonne?

I'm about to ask when Hunter starts to talk. "Do you ever check your phone?" he chides, his voice cold. "Do you have any idea why your mom has been trying to contact you?"

I stop short. "I had it on silent for class," I mutter, looking down at the screen. "I just assumed it was because of Medford—"

"Cameron Young escaped from prison today."

Cam.

For the third time today, it feels as though someone is pouring ice cold water over my head. My hands begin to shake as I look down at my phone, opening my texts. I have nine from my mom—long, block-like messages. One from Hunter that just asks where I am, and one from Andrew, asking to see me in his office.

Great.

I scan my mom's texts quickly. *Escaped, his friends in the department, not answering your phone, Medford...*

I swallow. "How?" I ask, looking up at Hunter.

Dark fury burns behind his eyes as he rolls his tongue around the inside of his cheek.

"Fuck if I know how the asshole did it." He inhales deeply. "I'm going to kill him, Briar."

I look down at the ground as my vision begins to tilt again. Ledger steps forward, showing me a news article from my old hometown on his phone—a mugshot of Cam below it.

Cameron Young, a former police officer in Marin County who was charged with rape earlier this year, escaped from San Quentin State Prison yesterday. The details of the escape are still under investigation. There is a $5,000 reward for anyone who finds him.

With shaky hands, I rub my eyes and sigh. "Fuck," I whisper, looking around nervously.

"Hey," Samson says, stepping forward. "We are going to keep you safe."

I look up at Hunter, and he nods. My eyes flick to Ledger, who just scowls, and then he pockets his phone.

Something comes over me then—something dark and menacing. I turn to Hunter again, clenching my fists.

"We have to find him." His eyes burn into mine, and Ledger and Samson stand next to Hunter, their arms crossed. "What's the alternative? We wait for the authorities to do their job? What if he..." I look down as tears prick at my eyes. "What if he finds us first?"

Ledger is the first to pull me into him, and his warm arms calm my racing heart.

"We'll find him," he murmurs into my hair, kissing the top of my head.

"But what if he hurts you?" I ask, my voice small against Ledger's broad chest. "I couldn't possibly ask you to help me with this. It's my mess," I finish.

They have futures—college applications, writing publications, school, notoriety, and familial reputations to uphold. I am a nobody. If anyone is going to put themselves at risk to find him, it should be me.

"There's no question that we're going to help you," Ledger answers, fisting my shirt and squeezing me tight. "All of us. We vowed to protect you, so we will do just that."

"Your ours to protect," Hunter agrees, smirking.

I pull away from Ledger, looking behind him at Samson—whose eyes bore into mine with fiery intensity.

"I will owe you my life," I whisper, looking at them.

"You," Hunter growls. "We just want you."

"You have all of me."

I make eye contact with each of them, so they know I mean all of us. Nine months ago, I had no one to turn to except my mom. I was called names and my story wasn't believed. But when I look into Ledger's blue eyes, when I see the fury roiling underneath the surface of his cruel smile, I know I'm safe. I can take care of myself but fighting against a crazed rapist will be a hell of a lot easier with four guys willing to risk everything for me—four guys willing to help me.

I've gone my entire life on my own. Fighting for peace after my trauma, fighting to fit in, fighting to be strong. I always had my boxing gloves on, always ready and on the defensive.

But as I look at the guys, I realize, they can help me take the gloves off. They can help me learn to depend on others again. They can help me—with their connections, their money, their reputation.

They can *help* me.

And I'm going to need all the help I can get taking Cam down.

35

Ash

I sigh, running my hands through my short hair. *This is such utter bullshit.* I glance at the guard pacing outside my cell. I know the chief received my video—one of the sergeants mentioned it in the interrogation. *So why am I still here?*

I stand and walk to the door, waiting for the guard to head back this way. I wish I could text Briar, the guys—update them. I didn't expect two officers to barge into my physics class, and I sure as hell didn't expect them to ask me to follow them outside. I didn't want to cause a scene, so I followed them—where they proceeded to arrest me on the hood of their car. Third period was in session, so only a couple of freshman girls on their way to the office saw me.

No doubt word will be out by now.

The guard walks up to the door and shakes his head. "It's for your own safety, Ash."

I glower at him, eventually kicking the bars, and he doesn't even flinch as he walks back toward the other end of the path.

Fuck this—fuck my dad.

According to the sheriff, I'm in deep shit for Medford—but my father is in deeper shit for punching me, and for the new investigation into my mom.

I swallow and look down at the cement, breathing heavily.

My mother and I are both prisoners in his world, and he wouldn't have it any other way.

I'm just about to ask to make a call when he wanders back over to the door, unlocking it.

"I guess it's your lucky day, Mr. Greythorn. We found your father, and he's in custody." He swings the door open, and I pause.

"What next?"

He shrugs. "Your bail has been paid. You just have to await a trial. Because your father is a danger to you, and because you're still in school, you can either arrange to stay with a family member or a friend, or we can contact social services."

I frown. "I'll figure it out."

He leads me out, and we stop by the property room to grab my cell phone, wallet, and keys. I sign some papers, including a requisite form showing where I'll be staying for the time being. I scribble down Hunter's address. He directs me to the exit.

"Who paid my bail?" I ask, pushing the door open as I unlock my phone.

He nudges his jaw to the black Range Rover waiting out front.

I smile as I walk over, and when I get closer, Briar throws the passenger door open.

"Let's fuck some shit up," she purrs, grinning.

36

BRIAR

Hunter drives us all back to our house, and fortunately, my mom's car is gone, which means both she and Andrew are out. He cuts the engine, and we exit. I unlock the door and look over at Hunter as he smirks.

It's still strange to know that we share a house together.

That this is *our* home.

We walk to the kitchen, and Ash grabs a beer from the fridge before we sit at the table.

I like this—that I'm a part of their exploitations. That they're including me in their plans.

"So, what are we going to do?" Samson asks, licking his lips. He has his hands clasped together, and he's watching us expectantly.

I shrug. "I don't know. Ash was the only one identified, so—"

"Briar," Ledger growls, his eyes fixed on my face. "He's not talking about Medford. He's talking about you."

My body goes cold. "That's why we're here? We're not making sure our stories about Medford are tight, that they align in case we're interrogated?"

Hunter turns in his chair and bends forward, placing his large, warm hands on my bare thighs. My body explodes with electricity.

"None of us give two shits about Medford, baby."

I swallow. "Oh. I just thought—"

"I'm going to fucking kill him," Ash declares, his voice edged with anger. He looks at me as he takes a swig of beer. "Skin him alive and make him eat his own flesh." His light blue eyes grow darker by the second as he sneers. "For what he did to you, he deserves much worse."

Shivers claw down my spine, one vertebra at a time. My breathing hitches. They're all looking at me, waiting.

Plotting.

I think of the guys I saw that first night in the park.

The guys who lit the house in the preserve on fire.

The guys everyone at Ravenwood Academy feared.

My heart pounds against my ribs as I realize they're waiting, ready to pounce.

For me.

I'm just about to ask what our options are when the front door closes. Hunter and I both hop up, and I breathe a sigh of relief when my mom walks through the arched doorway of the kitchen. She looks between Hunter and me, a bag of food in one hand, and a fountain soda in the other. I don't think I've ever seen her drink soda.

"Hi, honey," she says solemnly, setting her cup down

and sighing. She flicks her eyes to Hunter. "Can you please give us a minute?"

The guys stand up and walk out of the kitchen. Ash's eyes find mine just before he turns the corner. The rage is still blazing, and I realize with a start that Ash *will* kill Cam if given the chance.

I sit down and sigh. "Do they know the motive?" I ask, crossing my arms and leaning back.

She slides in next to me, putting an arm around my shoulders. "No, but it's not hard to guess," she starts, her voice low. When I look at her, tears begin to well in her eyes.

"I'm so, so sorry, Briar," she says, sniffling and pulling me into her. "I'm your mother. I was supposed to protect you."

I stiffen. "Mom, this wasn't your fault."

"He was my boyfriend. I thought—I thought he was safe," she whispers, swiping the tears that have begun to run down her face. "And I thought this mess was behind us."

I nod. "Me too."

"I can't believe he escaped San Quentin," she adds, her voice hard. "Someone must've helped him." She sighs. "But I want you to know that we're safe here, Briar."

I loosen in her arms, closing my eyes. "I know, Mom." *I have four guys willing to take a bullet for me...* "And I'm sorry about Medford."

I'd seen her ask about it in one of her texts this morning.

"One thing at a time," she murmurs, chuckling.

My eyes snap open and I pull away. "Why are you drinking soda?"

She waves my question away. "I don't know. I heard about Cam, and then Medford... stress eating," she laughs, shaking her head.

I rear my head back suspiciously, but before I can ask any more questions, the front door slams again.

"That's Andrew." We stand, and Andrew comes stalking into the kitchen. He's in his suit, having come straight from school. He walks right up to me.

"Briar," he says, relieved. He pulls me into a hug, and my throat constricts. Despite everything—despite not knowing me that well—I can tell he really cares about me. "I've spoken to my lawyers. I think we should hire our own investigators to find him."

"I agree," my mom chimes in, turning to me. "But it's up to you, hon."

I nod. "Yeah. Let's do it."

Let's take that motherfucker down.

☙❦❧

After Andrew, my mom, and I talk logistics and they head out to run some errands, I walk down to the basement, where I suspect the guys have been hanging out. As I land on the last stair and look into the room, I see only Hunter sitting on the couch. He's watching TV, but his eyes are unfocused.

Distracted.

They snap to mine as I walk over. Standing in front of him, I grab the remote from the couch, and he smirks.

"Rule number one," I murmur, turning the TV off. "No more wearing that uniform around me when you're at home." My eyes trail across the tight, white button-up he has rolled up to his elbows, and the navy slacks that fit his thighs like gloves. He's kicked his boots off, but it doesn't matter. He looks unkempt, yet...

Godly.

He smiles, spreading his legs and leaning forward, his hands clasped together as he rests his elbows on his knees.

"I suppose that should be a household rule," he utters, looking directly at me. He brushes his hand across my bare leg, his thumb trailing up the inside of my thigh. I shudder.

"Rule number two," I say, faltering slightly as his fingers move upwards and flick against the wetness pooling in my panties. "Help me get my revenge, and you can have me in whatever way you want."

It feels good to say it out loud. Because while a legal trial is fine, my idea of revenge is so, so much worse. I probably wasn't the first girl he raped. And I certainly won't be the last if he finds a way to remain under the radar.

We have to find him.

"That's far too tempting," he murmurs, pulling my thong to the side. "I can't decide if we're doing you a favor, or if you're doing us a favor."

"Neither," I whisper. "We're helping each other."

"You are ours," he says again, his other hand coming to the back of my skirt and lifting the material. He grips the flesh on my bare ass, squeezing. I let out a loud moan. "And we are yours. I think it's time the *Kings* of Ravenwood appoint a *Queen*."

My stomach lurches. "What?"

He bites his lower lip as he pulls me down onto his lap. I place both knees on either side of him so that I'm straddling him. I can feel his erratic heartbeat, and his throat bobs as he swallows. He unzips his pants and positions himself below me, moving the material of my undies to the side.

"Your ours now, Briar Monroe. Body, mind... and soul."

And then he thrusts into me, and I gasp, arching my back. "Oh, fuck," I whimper, shuddering. He fills me completely to the hilt, and my eyes flutter closed.

Yes. If this is what making a deal with the devil is like, I will sign everything I am—everything I ever was or will be—over to them.

They can have me.

I surrender.

"Say it, little lamb," Hunter commands, his hand on my shoulder, holding me low as he drives into me, his length as deep as it will go. "Say you're ours."

"I'm yours," I whisper without even thinking. "I've always been yours."

He groans and moves faster, his thick, hard cock hitting my cervix with every thrust. There's a deep ache—but it also feels incredible.

"Good girl," he grumbles, a thin sheen of sweat on his face as he works himself underneath me, holding me down.

Heat courses through me, and I move my hips to try to ride him, but his grip on my shoulders is strong.

He wants control.

I stay still as the pace quickens, breathing heavily and meeting Hunter's eyes as they blaze with lust and fury. He bares his teeth as he works harder, and the feeling of him so deep, of taking me fully, makes me delirious with pleasure. Our breathing quickens, and he begins to pump faster, nearing his climax.

"Come with me," he demands, squeezing my nipple between the material of my shirt.

Fuck.

I lean forward and kiss him, claiming him as much as he's claiming me. I may be theirs—but that means they are mine, too. Our lips work each other, slow and smooth, and he moans into my mouth, biting my lower lip as he begins to tremble.

It sends sparks through my body—feeling him harden, feeling him pulse inside of me. I fly over the edge with him.

"Oh, fuck," he says, his forehead touching mine as he empties into me, and I quiver in his arms as the last of it leaves my body. He's panting, and he holds my wrists down at my side as we both take steadying breaths.

I climb off him and hold my skirt up as he reaches into his pocket, cleaning me up with a handkerchief. We both stand, and he zips himself back up. I smooth my hair out, and once we're both presentable again, he takes my hand.

"Come on."

I grab my phone and let him pull me out of the room. "Where are we going?"

He chuckles, making sure we grab our things before we close the house up and head back to his car.

"Let's go make a spectacle out of you and introduce Ravenwood Academy to their new Queen."

37

Ledger

It's like she's made for this, like she's always been the fifth element to our group. I think of Plato, and how he came up with the notion of the rare fifth element—or what's known as an aether.

Rare.
Unknown.
Celestial.
Pure—purer than the other four elements.

The next day, exactly ten days after showing up at Ravenwood Academy, Briar parks next to us and unabashedly secures her position as the Queen of Ravenwood. And she does it so naturally, with a calm demeanor and a ruthless expression on her face as she positions herself directly in the middle of the four of us.

I know people expected it. I could tell she was already making a name for herself. But just how natural it feels, how she fits right into the lockstep, like our missing puzzle piece—*that* was unexpected on my part.

Our little lamb.

I find myself distracted most of the morning, zoning out and thinking about Medford, about how pliable she was in my arms. How I was ready to make her *feel something good,* how I wanted to fuck her senseless to get rid of the death permeating the surrounding air.

I walk into the locker room and change into my gym clothes, running my hands through my hair and grabbing a towel. It's sprint day, and though I love running, today I don't feel like withholding myself from Briar for fifty minutes while Coach screams at me. He seems to push me and ride me harder than the other students. Maybe because he knows I have a future in track.

Briar walks over to where the students are all grouped together, waiting for the coach to instruct them. I shield my face from the sun, wanting to be inside of her, and only her. He tells us to run sprints—100 meters, grouped by last name. I smile, knowing that means Briar will probably be with me. I saunter up to her as the first group begins.

"Remember to warm up," I instruct her, bouncing and running in place. Her hair is pulled back into a tight ponytail, and I like seeing her face bare of makeup like this.

She mimics me, jumping up and down as we jog in place together. As her tits bounce, my cock swells in my shorts.

"Want to race?" she says playfully, tilting her head.

Fuck me.

"You're going to lose," I chide, grinning.

"We'll see," she responds, furrowing her brows as we

walk up to our place on the start lines. I was right—it's Briar, me, and two other guys.

"And if I win?" I ask, bending over and getting ready for Coach's whistle.

Her eyes drift down to my shorts, and her eyebrows shoot up as she bites her lower lip and looks back up at me.

"Remember to warm up," she purrs, her voice low so that no one else can hear her.

My cock hardens, and I groan as Coach's whistle sounds.

I'm too distracted—and my dick doesn't allow me to move as quickly as I know I can. Briar sprints past me, and I push myself to catch up. The problem with 100 meters is that you don't have very long to redeem yourself, unless you want to work two, three, or even ten times harder to overpower the others.

She finishes just before I do.

"Fuck," I whisper, smiling.

She whoops her fist in the air, and then she walks up to me, her face flushed. "I won."

"Yeah, no shit," I mutter, adjusting my cock. "You had an unfair advantage."

She grins before flicking her eyes down to my shorts. "Did I?"

And then she walks away.

The rest of the class goes slower than molasses. By the time Coach dismisses us, I'm sweaty, rock hard, and fidgety. I try to calm down for a few minutes, waiting until the other guys are done showering, so they don't see my hard on while I rinse off.

When the shower room is finally empty, I strip and

grab a towel, wrapping it around my waist as I walk to the small, tiled room with four showerheads.

"I'd give it a nine," a voice sounds from behind me just as I let the first drops of hot water run down my body.

I'd know that low, light timber anywhere. I glance over my shoulder, smiling, and see Briar standing at the other end of the shower room.

Naked.

38

BRIAR

It was advantageous of me to even attempt to beat Ledger at the sprint. But did I expect to beat him? Absolutely not. And I couldn't help but sneak into the boy's locker room to see if he was still there—and he was.

Alone, naked, and *mine*.

I admire the way the water runs down his tanned, naked body. His back is to me, and his ass is chiseled and firm, with little dips on the top of his hips that accentuate his muscular back. I don't think he has an ounce of fat on him. Just muscles wrapped in thick, black ink. It runs down his arms, forming two half-sleeves, and inward onto his back and chest. His hair is slicked back and wet, and he grins at me with that perfectly straight, white smile as he finishes rinsing his body off. When he turns around, my mouth goes dry. His cock is already hard, tilted upward and thick against his stomach.

"Are you coming in here, or do I have to throw you over my shoulder and drag you in?"

There's no doubt that he could—he is tall, nearly a foot taller than me, and his muscle mass alone makes him twice my size. I slowly walk over, and his eyes rake over my body once—twice. His eyes narrow as he turns to face me fully.

"Aren't you the little daredevil," he purrs, and as he reaches out for me, I drop to my knees. "Well, well, well," he adds, smirking.

"Shut up," I counter, and then I take his length and stroke it with my hand. He moans, unconsciously thrusting into my hand as water runs down his body. I smile up at him. "Out of all the things that happened to me since being here, you stealing my clothes was the most mortifying. Maybe that's why I made you wait—why you're the last one I'm going to fuck."

He chuckles. "I was just teasing you," he replies, and before he can say anything else, I open my mouth and take him in as deep as I can. "Holy shit," Ledger growls, his voice hoarse as I work my lips along his veiny shaft, allowing his thick head to hit the back of my throat with every thrust.

I use one hand to stroke him and the other to play with his balls. Sweating from the steam, I moan as his dick twitches, and he grabs my wet hair and forces himself deeper. I gag but I don't show it.

"Deeper," he grunts, panting. "You look so fucking good sucking my cock, little lamb."

I moan into him, quickening my pace and taking him as deep as physically possible. My eyes water, but the notion of nearly swallowing him whole makes me wet. I take the hand on his balls and move it between my legs, circling my clit with two fingers as I work him, squeezing my eyes shut.

"I want to come all over your tits," he murmurs, groaning as he squeezes my hair. "I'm getting close. I've been thinking of your tight, little pussy all week long."

I moan and quicken the pace on myself. Sparks fly down my limbs, and wetness drips down my legs as I listen to him breathe fast and loud. My core tightens as my climax begins to build, and just as I'm about to come, he cries out.

"Fuck, I'm going to come so soon," he hisses.

I look up at him through my wet lashes, and his cock hardens further. He's so close to exploding in my mouth. Which is why the next thing I do is so fun. I pull off quickly and stand, wiping my mouth before I cross my arms. "I lied. You're like a six."

If I could bottle up the startled expression on his pretty face, I would. I just smile and turn to walk away.

"You think I'm going to let you walk away after that?" he growls, and before I can brace myself, he's behind me, his wet, hot body against my back and dragging me back to the shower.

I'm laughing as he drops down to his knees and pulls my hips to his mouth roughly.

"You sure you don't want to run away screaming?" he murmurs, referencing the night at Medford. His chin is on my stomach, and my heart leaps into my throat. He grips my bare ass with his rough fingers.

"No," I whisper, fisting his hair and pulling his head back a little. "But like I said before, you don't scare me."

He hums in satisfaction before bending down and *feasting*. Because that's what he does—he flicks his tongue between my slit, devouring me. And holy fuck. I'd forgotten about the tongue ring until now. It knocks against my clit, causing my hips to buck and my legs to quake from the intensity. I cry out loudly as the warm metal slides against my nub, and his tongue tries to swallow me whole.

"God, you taste like fucking honey," he growls, inserting two fingers as he slides back and forth against my clit forcefully.

"Oh, fuck!" I cry, throwing my head back as my knees wobble. I grip the shower control—something to hold on to—and fiery sparks begin to go off in my core and run down my arms and legs. My hair is matted to my face, the stream of the shower making his hands slip and slide between my legs. I look up for just a second, and I still, my heart leaping into my throat.

Hunter is leaning against the shower room entrance, watching with dark amusement. His lips quirk up in the corners when he sees me notice him, and he nods once. I look down at Ledger, but he doesn't notice his friend. As I look back up at Hunter, he just holds a finger in front of his mouth as he unbuckles his pants.

Holy shit.

I fist Ledger's hair harder, and he moans into me, causing the vibrations to roll through me. Hunter whips his cock out, stroking it quickly as he watches Ledger go down on me.

"Fuck," I whisper, my whole body tingling and on fire.

"Come for me, Briar," Ledger demands, thrusting his tongue against me. He pulls back for a second. "I need you to come for me now. The next class will be in here any minute."

He's right—though the shower room is separate from the main locker room, *anyone* could walk in and see us. Just like Hunter did.

My eyes snap to my stepbrother, and he has a serious, concentrated look on his face as he thrusts his hips into his hand rhythmically. I remember how he felt underneath me, how his face contorted ever so slightly as he came, as he let me ride him until I was full...

I fall over the edge quickly, my legs shaking as Ledger grabs both ass cheeks and dips his tongue ever so deeply. I groan and shatter on top of his face, watching Hunter as he sprays the floor with come, twitching as the last of it leaves his body. He winks and zips his pants up before turning to go.

Ledger slaps my ass, standing and kissing me intensely on the lips. Pulling away, he smiles.

"Get to class, little lamb," he murmurs, handing me a towel and pushing me away gently.

I wrap myself up and he does the same, but it barely disguises the hard erection poking through the thin material.

"You don't want to..." I look around.

He laughs and runs a hand through his wet hair. "Despite what my friends might consider a good shag, I know better, and your time is coming," he adds, his eyes hooded as he bends down and gives me a gentle kiss on the lips. "The first time I fuck you will not be in a school locker room."

I blush and grab my clothes as we exit the shower room. To my horror, several guys are standing around and talking before P.E. They go silent as Ledger and I walk through, and one of them looks particularly surprised, so I wink at him. He blushes, and I smile as Ledger leads me to the girls' locker room. Once we're about to go our separate ways, he tilts his head and dips his fingers in his mouth, walking backward. Slowly licking them, he grins.

"Like honey."

39

BRIAR

That night, after I spend three hours catching up on homework, I find my mom furiously scrubbing the kitchen sink. I wrap my arms around her. She pivots and pulls me into a tight hug, kissing my forehead.

"Everything's going to be okay, you know that, right?"

I nod, suddenly *so* exhausted.

It's been *go, go, go* since my first day at Ravenwood. I haven't had a chance to process or even catch my breath. The drama is high, and the sex is... tiring.

I sigh as she brushes a strand of hair out of my face. As I open my mouth to say something, I realize up close that she's not wearing makeup. She doesn't necessarily wear a lot, but she has an everyday look that consists of mascara and blush, at least. She hardly ever starts her day without it.

"Are you okay?" I ask, pulling away.

Her eyes widen, and she puts a hand on her hip. "Of course." She's in sweatpants and a loose T-shirt. She never stays this casual—usually only on Christmas, or if she's sick…

Something's going on.

"Are you sick?" I ask, crossing my arms. "The sleeping in, the soda, no makeup, *sweatpants*," I screech, laughing. "What's going on?"

I see it then—her giving in to whatever is ailing her. She looks *exhausted*. Running a hand through her hair, she sighs, giving me a small smile.

"I'm pregnant."

My vision tilts slightly, and I grab on to the counter. "What?"

"I found out the week before we moved. I didn't say anything, because I wanted to give you time to settle in, but…" She puts a hand over her mouth. "I am having the *worst* morning sickness, and it's getting to be impossible to hide," she confesses.

I laugh and pull her into a hug, making sure I'm gentle. "This is amazing news! I'm going to have a brother or a sister?"

She nods, and then she starts to cry. "I'm sorry, I'm just an emotional mess," she sobs, wiping her cheeks. "You and Hunter are going to have a little brother or sister."

Her words bolt through me, and I frown.

Oh, fuck.

The thought of sharing a sibling with Hunter—despite us not sharing blood—somehow makes what we're doing so much worse. I hug my mom again, squeezing my eyes shut. I think of earlier, in the shower room—watching him stroke himself, making eye contact as Ledger devoured me—and I suddenly feel so guilty.

"This is really exciting," I manage to say. "Can I help with anything?" I shoo her away from the sink. "You shouldn't be using all of these chemicals," I chide, shaking my head at the bleach she's using the scour the porcelain sink.

She laughs. "I cleaned with you, and you turned out fine, hon."

Did I?

"Andrew knows, right?" I ask, putting the gloves on and rinsing off the white foam.

"Yep. We weren't trying, but I guess life's funny like that."

It sure is.

We chat for a few more minutes before she excuses herself to go take a nap. *Pregnant.* My mom is pregnant, and that baby will be related to both Hunter and me. Before, we had no blood connection, so we could justify what we were doing. But now? We'll be tethered together by a sibling forever. And if things don't work out with him...

I finish cleaning the kitchen, and then I pull my phone out of my hoodie pocket. I want to tell my friends, but instead, I shoot a quick text to Sonya. She doesn't respond, and I chew on the inside of my cheek as I draft a text to Scarlett and Jack. I didn't see them at school the second half of yesterday, and they made themselves scarce today. A pang of guilt rolls through me when I think of them, how they took me under their wings on my very first day without question. And what did I do? Make a fool of myself? I know I wasn't identified on camera at Medford, but the rumor is already out.

They know I was there because they know I left the party with them.

I delete the long text I have drafted, instead dialing Scarlett's number. She picks up on the fourth ring.

"I almost didn't pick up," she mumbles.

I smile. "Thank you for changing your mind."

"What do you want, Briar?"

"I just want to apologize," I answer, chewing on a hangnail. "I didn't mean for you guys to find out the way you did, and I know how stupid it was to vandalize Medford Asylum. I just... got caught up in the moment, I guess."

She's quiet for a few seconds, and then she sighs. "They have questionable morals. And truthfully, I feel like they're taking advantage of you. Like maybe you have Stockholm Syndrome."

I try not to snort. "Scarlett, it's not like that at all, I promise. I think their reputation precedes them." I pause. "Something... terrible happened to me in California. They've been nothing but helpful since finding out. They talk the talk, but they're mostly harmless."

"Yeah, well, Micah said the exact same thing."

Goosebumps rise on my skin, making the hairs stand up on my arms. "His situation was different," I mutter.

"Was it? Because I'm trying to find the differences and I can't. Except you now have four guys sharing you... Mind you, I am all for polyamory, but you really think they won't fight to the death for you? If you're going to be in a relationship with multiple guys, at least make sure they're decent human beings."

I swallow. "No, they're not like that. I promise. The situation with Micah was—"

"Whatever, Briar. Honestly, I just need a few days to cool down. I really like you. I don't want to lose you as a friend. But it's hard watching a friend go down this path, with seemingly no care in the world. I did it once, and I won't do it again."

And then she hangs up, leaving me to feel like the most worthless pile of shit ever.

Hunter doesn't come home until after midnight, just as I'm climbing into bed. He knocks on my door gently, and I smile as he walks in.

His eyes rove over my body, scantily clad in my new silk pajamas, and he leans against the door frame. He's in jogging pants and a sweatshirt.

"Out with the guys?" I ask, fluffing my pillow.

He shakes his head. "I went on a run."

I smirk. "All night?"

He stares at me. "Yes. I had a lot on my mind. Cam, Medford, you, our new sibling..." He sighs. So, Andrew told him about the baby... "I can't seem to let you go, Briar. You're infiltrating every aspect of my life. And now our parents are having a baby, and that ties us together forever."

I cross my arms. "Does that scare you?"

He watches me for a beat before walking in, shutting the door behind him. My pulse quickens as he makes his way over to my bed.

"No, it doesn't scare me," he murmurs, sitting down

next to me. "I'm not afraid of having you in my life forever. I'm afraid of losing you." I swallow as he moves closer. "Lie down," he commands, nudging his jaw toward the bed.

"Are you going to tuck me in?" I tease, climbing underneath the covers.

His expression is dead serious as he answers, "Yes."

And then he does—wrapping the thick duvet around me, kissing me on the lips for a split second, and then turning the light out. Walking to the door, he pauses.

"Goodnight, Briar."

I smile into the duvet. "Goodnight, Hunter."

40

SAMSON

There's nothing I hate more than waiting in line at the grocery store. The food sitting in my basket, the ice cream thawing, the meat warming up... Frankly, it's disgusting. So, as I wait behind a burly man in a hat, his cart full to the brim, I sigh.

Of course this would be my luck.

I crane my neck and look for another available cashier, but the one in my lane seems to be the only one.

Awesome.

I pull my phone out and fidget on social media. I shoot a quick text to Briar, since she's coming over for dinner later. That's why I'm here. My parents have been out of town at a doctor's conference, so I have the house—and Briar—to myself.

I accidentally drop the pack of Skittles I'm holding, and it smacks against the linoleum loudly.

The man in front of me turns and smiles, reaching down and picking them up.

"Here," he whispers, handing me the red bag and winking.

I don't—can't—say thank you.

It registers slowly at first because I can't think of how I know him. Then, the recognition slams into me—I must be dreaming. *Cam.* I stared at his mugshot for far too long not to recognize him. I will my face into neutrality, giving him a small smile before he turns back around.

There's only one reason he's here—and all that food is not for a quick trip across the county.

He's here—and it looks like he's here to stay.

I mutter an excuse about feeling sick, abandoning my cart completely as I exit the store.

41

Briar

I pace around the basement as Samson wrings his hands together.

"He was just... buying food?" I ask for the millionth time.

My mom and Andrew don't know yet. They're at some sort of private ultrasound place, and I don't want to ruin their exciting day. They have the future to look forward to—a new baby, a new life, a new city...

And yet, my past is haunting me as we speak.

"He's obviously here because of you," Samson says, checking his phone for the hundredth time. He called the guys right after he told me in person. They're on their way. "I should've killed him, right then and there," Samson mutters, leaning back and shaking his head.

"That would be murder," I joke.

He leans forward and watches me through his glasses, his eyes twinkling. "I think you should do it."

I still. "Do what? Kill him?"

Before he can answer, I hear a stampede on the stairs, and a second later, Hunter, Ash, and Ledger are all before me.

Waiting.

"So, what's the plan?" Hunter asks, sitting down in front of me. "As much as I want to kill him, I think we should notify the police. Soon, before he runs."

I shrug. Ash and Ledger sit next to him, and they're all watching me.

"If he's here, he obviously doesn't want me to know right away," I start. "That gives me an advantage." I swallow. "I don't think he's going to run. He's not here by some coincidence."

Ash sneers. "I think you should kill him. Gut him from end to end."

"Jesus," Ledger says, laughing. "Calm down, Hannibal Lecter." He turns to face me. "What if we fuck with him a bit first?"

Samson tilts his head. "I don't hate that idea, either. You could trick him. Lure him into a trap, and then you'd be five grand richer."

"I'd rather not go near him in any way," I respond, my body rejecting the idea of ever getting that physically close to Cam again.

"Briar," Hunter murmurs, standing behind me. "What do *you* want to do?" he mutters, brushing the hair off my neck before kissing me there. I think of the house in the preserve—of Medford.

Of that itch to get revenge.

I shiver as his lips caress my skin. Ash stands next and stops right in front of me. "Let us help you," he murmurs, dropping to his knees.

I gasp as he licks the bare skin between my shorts and shirt.

Ledger walks over and stands next to Ash, running his hands through my hair before trailing a calloused thumb along my jaw.

Samson is last—taking his time as he stands on the other side of Ash. He brings his lips down to my ear. "I think we all want to see you mess with him—see you show him just how strong you are, despite what the motherfucker did to you."

I begin to tremble uncontrollably, and I'm not sure if it's because they're all here, all touching me somehow, or if it's the thought—the fear—of possibly seeing Cam again.

"Our brave, little lamb," Hunter adds. "He thinks he can get away with ambushing you," he growls, and the others chime in. "But he has no idea how formidable you really are."

Me.

I'm *formidable*.

But that's how they think—that's how they treat me. Like I'm strong, like I can do this, like I'm something to be revered.

Like a Queen.

I throw my head back as hands work my body, and after a few seconds, I'm not sure who is who, but my body is on fire.

No.

I can't get carried away.

My eyes snap open. "We have to make a plan. A smart one. Something he won't see coming."

It makes me sick that Cam is here. Whatever ulterior motive he has can't be good.

"Briar," Hunter purrs from behind me. "Just tell us what to do."

My eyes flutter closed briefly as Ash's tongue flicks against the skin on my stomach.

"Help me," I whisper. "I can't do it alone."

"Yes, you can," Samson whispers, his breath on my neck. "You can do it alone. But you don't have to."

I pull my lower lip into my mouth, humming. They are here. They are going to help me. I feel my chest constrict at the thought—at how they started as my worst nightmare but will ultimately be my saving grace. My worst enemies will become my biggest support system. But that means I am indebted to them.

"I owe you," I say, my voice uneven. "All of you."

Ash stands, reaching into his pocket for something. I still when I see it's a knife.

"An oath," he murmurs, slicing his palm. "To protect you."

"Jesus," Hunter mutters. "What the fuck, man?"

Ash grins. "Blood for blood," he muses.

Hunter, Ledger, and Samson all hold their hands out reluctantly, and Ash slices their flesh a little too easily for my liking. Then, he turns to me.

"You are ours. Body and soul. Whenever we want you, *however* we want you."

My throat goes dry. "And you are mine," I purr.

I hold my hand out, palm up, and he cuts me. I grit my

teeth as the blood pools, and then I shake each of their hands.

Making a deal with the devil is one thing.

But making a deal with four?

I smile.

What the hell have I gotten myself into?

TO BE CONTINUED...

You can preorder book 2, Ruthless Queen, below! It releases on September 14, 2021.

Ruthless Queen

Hunter, Ash, Ledger, and Samson.
The Kings of Ravenwood Academy.
Their names still send shivers down my spine, for more than one reason.

Back then, they didn't expect me to fight back.
But I did.
And now I'm theirs.

After making a pact with them, they help me get revenge on the one man who wronged me.
I'm not the same meek, little girl that got taken advantage of.

Now, I have four ruthless guys willing to risk everything for me.
The only problem is, I promised them everything I had in return for their help.

So while I may be the new Queen of Ravenwood, the Kings still own me, body and soul.
And I'm not quite sure I'm ready to hand over my crown.

Ruthless Queen is full-length high-school bully reverse harem romance. It is book two of the Ruthless Royals duet. It is advised to read them in order. *Please note Ruthless Queen contains explicit language, bullying, violence, and flashbacks of abuse/trauma. It also features four hot AF guys who would do anything to protect their feisty Queen. The story concludes with this book and does have a HEA.

Preorder Now!

Also, don't forget to sign up for my mailing list! There are monthly giveaways, exclusive excerpts, and I share news there before anywhere else! It's the best place to keep in touch with me. *I also have something fun in the works later this year for my subscribers!

Mailing List

ACKNOWLEDGMENTS

I suppose I should start at the beginning, when I randomly stumbled upon these covers online, and instantly knew I had to have them. I didn't have a story yet, and they sat for a few months until I was driving one night and the entire plot of this book flooded into my mind. And that's how the Ruthless Royals duet was born. So, thank you Emma Rider for these gorgeous covers. They inspired an entire duet!

Thank you to my husband, Peter. Your comments and advice helped shape a lot of this story, and I'm grateful you took the time to read it (twice!) I'm sorry my screen is so bright when you're trying to sleep, lol.

To the Nerd Herd—thank you for encouraging me to write something outside of my comfort zone. I know how excited you are for this story, and it was your excitement that got me through those moments that had me second guessing myself.

To Traci Finlay, for the diligent editing. As always with you, this story is ten times better now thanks to your suggestions, edits, and comments.

To my author friends, specifically the ones who helped shape this story in some way, even if you didn't know it—R Holmes, Brianna Hale, Sara Cate, Hollis Wynn, Elizabeth Dear, Kate Farlow, and so many more. Thank you for the DMs, the cover excitement, the blurb critiques, and for letting me vent when I thought this story was the worst thing I've ever written.

To Callie Rae, who sat through a panicked phone call with me when I thought I'd never whip this story into shape. Thanks for taking the time to talk me off a ledge. You are incredible!

To Shelbe, I'm so glad we "met" on TikTok! Thank you for customizing bookmarks for me, for taking the time to make incredible teasers and graphics, and for generally being so supportive of me and my writing.

To my boys, for being adorable menaces. Where would I be without you? More rested, probably, but I cannot imagine doing this life without your cute, little faces by my side.

And last but not least, my readers. Whether you found me from a silly TikTok video or you've been here since Evi and Nick... whew! It's been a wild ride. Thank you so much for being here. I would not be doing this without your comments, messages, and emails.

ABOUT THE AUTHOR

Amanda Richardson writes from her chaotic dining room table in Los Angeles, often distracted by her husband and two adorable sons. When she's not writing contemporary and dark, twisted romance, she enjoys coffee (a little too much) and collecting house plants like they're going out of style.

You can visit my website here: www.authoramandarichardson.com

Facebook: http://www.facebook.com/amandawritesbooks

For news and updates, please sign up for my newsletter here!

ALSO BY AMANDA RICHARDSON

Love at Work Series:

Between the Pages

A Love Like That

Tracing the Stars

Say You Hate Me

HEATHENS Series (Dark Romance):

SINNERS

HEATHENS

MONSTERS

VILLAINS (coming 2022)

Standalones:

The Realm of You

The Island

Ruthless Royals Duet (Reverse Harem):

Ruthless Crown

Ruthless Queen

Printed in Great Britain
by Amazon